Compact Classics

The Adventures of Tom Sawyer

Mark Twain

Abridged and simplified by
S. E. Paces

Ward Lock Educational

WARD LOCK EDUCATIONAL CO., LTD.
T R House, 1 Christopher Road, East Grinstead,
Sussex RH19 3BT, England.

A member of the Ling Kee Group
London · Hong Kong · New York · Singapore

ISBN 0 7062 4938 0

The Adventures of Tom Sawyer
adapted by S. E. Paces was first published
in Hong Kong by Ling Kee Publishing Co. Ltd, 1970.

This edition © Ward Lock Educational 1989

Questions and discussion points compiled by Jill Cooke.

Printed in Hong Kong

Contents

Introduction

Mark Twain (1835–1910) is one of the most popular American writers of the nineteenth century. He came from a poor family, and left school at the age of thirteen to work as a printer. In his leisure time, he wrote stories for a local newspaper.

At the age of twenty, Mark Twain began to work on a boat which sailed up and down the Mississippi River. It was here that he met the characters he describes in his books. He was a brilliant storyteller and many of his tales are about his journeys on the Mississippi and life in the American south.

The Adventures of Tom Sawyer is the best known of Twain's books. It was written in 1876 and describes the boyhood of Tom Sawyer, an orphan who lives with his kind Aunt Polly. Tom is a cheerful, honest, lively boy. His adventures have delighted boys and girls all over the world.

If you like *The Adventures of Tom Sawyer*, you will also enjoy *The Adventures of Huckleberry Finn*. There you will find many of the characters you meet in this book.

1

THIS IS TOM SAWYER!

"*Tom!*"

No answer.

"Tom!"

No answer.

"Where can he be?" *Aunt Polly* asked herself. "He must be somewhere here."

She went to the door, looked out into the garden and then shouted again, "Tom! Tom!"

No answer.

The old lady stood there thoughtfully. Suddenly she heard a sound behind her. She turned round quickly. There was Tom − near the cupboard door. There was jam all round his mouth!

"What have you been doing?" Aunt Polly asked angrily. When Tom did not answer, she went on, "You've been stealing the jam again. Don't tell me that you haven't! Haven't I told you a hundred times to keep away from that cupboard? Where's my stick?" Aunt Polly took her stick and raised it high. She was ready to strike Tom hard.

"Look behind you, Auntie!" shouted Tom.

Aunt Polly looked behind her. This was Tom's chance. He rushed out of the house. He climbed over the fence. Soon he was far away!

Aunt Polly was angry but she had to laugh. "He's a bad boy," she said to herself. "But I love him. He's my poor dead sister's boy, and I must look after him. I don't like to hit him, but I have to. If I don't punish him, he'll grow up lazy and wicked. Yes, I must be strict." Aunt Polly sighed. "I'll have to punish him for stealing the jam. But how? I know, tomorrow is Saturday and there's no school on Saturdays. The boys have a holiday. But I'll make Tom work. That will punish him."

Tom ran away from school that afternoon. It was a lovely day and so he went to the woods with his friend *Joe Harper*. They had a good time there, playing "Cowboys and Indians". He went home late that evening. When he went in, his aunt and his brother *Sid* were having their supper. His aunt felt certain that Tom had not been to school. She did not say so but she began asking him questions like this. "It was hot in school this afternoon, wasn't it, Tom?"

"Yes, Auntie, rather hot."

"You wanted to go swimming, didn't you?"

"No Auntie, not really."

"Let me look at your collar . . . . . ," Aunt Polly said this because she used to sew Tom's collar together so that he could not take his shirt off. Then, of course, he could not go swimming. Aunt Polly examined Tom's collar. It was still sewn together.

"Ah!" she cried, "You didn't go swimming. You're a good boy, Tom."

"Aunt Polly," said Sid, "you sewed his collar with white thread and now the thread is black. Look!"

Tom jumped up from the table and ran outside. He shouted over his shoulder to his brother, "I'll fight you for that!" He was angry with Sid. He was also angry with himself. "Sometimes she uses white thread and sometimes she uses black. Why didn't I notice that?" he was thinking.

Suddenly he saw in front of him a boy who was new to the village. Tom had never seen this boy before. The boy looked very strange to Tom. He was wearing fine clothes, and he had shoes on. Tom wore shoes only on Sundays, and he did not like them. He did not like this new boy either.

"I can knock you down," he said to the boy.

"Try!"

"I can if I want to!"

"You can't!"

"I can!"

"You can't!"

"I tell you I can!"

For a moment there was a pause. Both boys were breathing hard. Then Tom asked, "What's your name?"

"I shan't tell you."

"I can knock you down with one hand!"

"Try it! You say you can do it. But you can't. You're afraid!"

"Who's afraid?"

"You are!"

"I'm not!"

"You are!"

The two boys looked at each other very angrily. They moved nearer each other. Now their shoulders were touching. Both boys began pushing. They pushed each other hard. Then they stopped for a moment. With his big toe, Tom drew a line in the dust. "If you step over that line, I'll fight you!" he said. The new boy at once stepped over the line. The next moment, the two boys started fighting. They fought like two wild cats — hitting, kicking, and scratching each other. Both were on the ground now, rolling in the dust.

Their clothes were torn and dirty. Their noses were bleeding. Tom was the stronger of the two. At last he sat on the new boy. "Have you had enough?" he asked.

The boy did not answer. He tried hard to stand up. Tom hit him again. At last the boy cried "Enough!" Then Tom let him get up. The boy began to walk away. With one hand he was brushing the dust from his clothes. With the other he was holding his handkerchief to his nose. Tom stood there, laughing at him. The new boy then picked up a stone and threw it at Tom. Tom ran after him but he could not catch him. The new boy ran home. Tom waited for some time outside his house. He waited there till the boy's mother came out. "Go away!" she shouted. "You're a bad, wicked boy!"

Tom slowly walked home. When Aunt Polly saw his clothes, she was very angry. "You've been fighting again," she said. "Very well, I shall punish you. Tomorrow you'll have to work hard. No swimming for you tomorrow! No playing either!"

2

HOW TOM WHITEWASHED THE FENCE

The next day was Saturday. The school was shut. All the boys in the village were free. It was a beautiful day. The sun was shining. The birds were singing. The trees and flowers looked so fresh and lovely. Tom, of course, wanted to go swimming. All the other boys were going.

Tom came sadly out of the house. In one hand he held a long brush. In the other he carried a bucket which was full of whitewash. His aunt was making him whitewash the fence. Tom looked sadly at the fence. "How high it is! How long it is!" he thought. Indeed the height of the fence was nine feet and its length was thirty yards. Tom put his brush into the whitewash. He drew it slowly across the fence. It made a very small white mark. Tom tried again. Another very small white mark. Tom sat down. He sighed heavily.

Then Tom saw *Jim*. Jim was the boy who helped his aunt with the rougher work of the house. Jim was carrying a bucket. He was going to fetch some water from the village pump. "The other boys will be there at the pump," thought Tom. "Fetching water is hard work but it's better than whitewashing." So he called, "Jim! Let me fetch the water while you whitewash the fence!" "Oh no!" replied Jim. "The old lady said that I mustn't help you. She said that you must do the whitewashing yourself."

"I'll give you a marble, Jim, if you let me fetch the water." "A marble! Let me see it!"

Tom held out the marble in his hand. Jim looked at it. He put down his bucket. He took the marble. But Aunt Polly was close behind him. She hit him hard with her shoe. Jim quickly picked up the bucket and went running down the street. Tom picked up his brush and began working hard. Aunt Polly went back into the house.

Tom soon stopped working. He sat down again. He took out all the things that he had in his pockets. He had some marbles, some pieces of string and two or three broken toys. "No one will whitewash the fence for these," he thought. "No! I must think of a better plan." He thought and thought. Soon he had an idea.

He picked up his brush again. Again he began working hard. *Ben Rogers* was coming down the street. Tom pretended not to see him. He worked harder than ever. Ben was eating an apple. He looked very happy. He was pretending that he was a big ship, and he was rolling like one. He was giving orders in a loud voice, and the ship was obeying them. He came up to Tom. He rubbed his eyes. "Why! Tom," he cried in great surprise, "you're working!"

Tom said nothing. He went on with his whitewashing. He looked very interested in his work.

"Tom! You're working!" Ben repeated.

"Oh! It's you, Ben. I didn't notice you."

"I'm just going for a swim. You don't want to come, do you? You like working, don't you?"

"This isn't work," Tom said quietly, and he went on whitewashing.

"Not work!" Ben exclaimed.

"Oh no! I like it. Whitewashing is fun. You've never whitewashed a fence, have you?"

"Well, no! I haven't."

For a time, Ben stood there watching Tom. Tom paid no attention to him. All his attention was given to his work. At last Ben said, "Let me whitewash a little!"

"Oh, no, Ben! I'm going to make this fence look fine. I've promised Aunt Polly. Besides, it's interesting."

"Let me do just a little," begged Ben.

"No! I'm sorry, Ben, but I can't. Aunt said that I must do it myself. If you do it, you'll make a mistake. You'll spoil everything. It's looking so nice now."

"I shan't make a mistake. I'll be careful. You can have my apple if you let me!"

Slowly and unwillingly, Tom handed the brush to Ben. Ben worked hard. He soon grew hot, but he went on working. Tom sat there, watching and eating Ben's apple.

When Ben had done enough, other boys came along. At first they laughed at Tom, as Ben had done. But soon they were whitewashing the fence. Of course they had to pay Tom before he let them help him. They gave him their best things — twelve marbles, a tin soldier, a key, a dog's collar, the handle of a knife and four pieces of orange. Tom had a lazy time. He did no work but soon the fence had three coats of whitewash on it!

Tom had learned something important that day. He had discovered two important laws. The first was: If a man *must* do something hard, then that is work. If he *likes* to do something hard, then that is not work. The second law was: If we cannot get something, we want it badly. If we can get something easily, we do not want it.

3

TOM IS BOTH HAPPY AND SAD

When the whitewashing was finished, Tom went indoors to tell his aunt.

"May I go out to play now?" he asked.

"How much whitewashing have you done?"

"All of it. The fence is quite finished."

"Finished? Let me see!"

Aunt Polly went outside to see. She was very surprised. She could hardly believe her eyes.

"Well, Tom," she said, "you've worked well. You can work when you want to. But it's not often that you want to, is it? All right; go and play. But don't be late home!" Aunt Polly smiled at Tom very kindly. She fetched the best apple from her cupboard and gave it to him.

Tom ran off. In the street he met Sid. He threw some stones at him. Then he ran on to the village. Most of his friends were there. The boys divided themselves into two armies. Tom was the captain of one army. His friend Joe Harper was the leader of the other. The two armies had a fierce battle. In the end, Tom's army won. Then the boys began to feel hungry and they went home.

On his way home, Tom passed the new boy's house. Tom looked over the fence into the garden. He did not see his enemy there but he saw a lovely girl. "She's more beautiful than *Amy Lawrence*. She's the loveliest girl in the world," Tom thought. He stood there, watching her for some time. The girl did not look at him. Then she moved slowly towards the house. When she reached the front door, she suddenly turned. She threw a rose over the fence to Tom. Tom ran and picked the rose up. Then he put it carefully inside his coat. He waited for the girl to appear again. It grew dark but she did not come out again. Tom walked home slowly and thoughtfully.

When he got home, he found his aunt angry with him. She was angry because he had thrown stones at Sid. Besides this, he had stolen some sugar from her cupboard. "Sid's a better boy than you are," she said to Tom. She went into the kitchen to get something. When she had gone, Sid put out his hand to take some sugar. He knocked the sugar-basin off the table. It fell with a crash to the floor. There it lay in pieces! "Ah!" thought Tom, "Now Aunt Polly will see whether Sid is better than I am." His aunt, hearing the crash, came running in. When she saw the broken basin, she went straight to Tom and hit him hard.

"Why are you hitting me? I didn't do it," Tom said.

"Be quiet! You're a bad boy all the same," Aunt Polly said.

Tom felt sorry for himself. "She'll be sorry about this when I'm dead," he thought. "But it'll be too late then." This thought was a sad one. It made Tom cry.

After a time, Tom got up and walked out of the house. He was thoughtful. His thoughts were sad ones. He sat down on the bank of the river. He took out his rose. He looked at his rose. He looked at it sadly. "Is that girl cruel too?" he asked himself, "Or is she different?"

Tom walked to her house. It was quite dark but in one window, a light was shining. Was she there? He climbed over the fence. He walked towards the window. In his hand he held the rose that she had thrown to him. "Ah!" he thought, "I wish I could die now, here under her window. She will find me here. But I shall be dead. What will she say then? Will she cry for me?"

Suddenly a window was opened. Somebody threw a lot of water on Tom's head. Perhaps they thought that Tom was a cat! Tom ran home.

4

TOM IS "DYING"!

It was Monday morning. Tom hated Mondays. School began on Monday and after that, there was a whole week of school. Tom hated going to school. He lay in bed, thinking ...... If he were ill, he would not have to go to school. But he was not ill. That was a pity! His head felt all right. His stomach felt all right. He had a loose tooth and that hurt him sometimes. If he told his aunt about it, she would pull it out at once. No, he could not stay at home for his tooth. What could he do? Then he remembered something. A week before, he had cut his toe. Perhaps it was poisoned. If it were poisoned, that would be serious. That would keep him at home.

Tom began to groan. He groaned louder and louder. Sid did not wake up. He groaned louder still. Sid slept on. Then Tom cried, "Sid! Sid! Wake up. I'm dying." He groaned again.

"What's the matter, Tom?" Sid asked. "Shall I fetch Auntie?"

"No, don't. I'll be better soon." Tom groaned again.

"Don't groan like that, Tom! How long have you been like this?"

"All night. But it doesn't matter. I know I'm dying. I'm glad to die. I forgive you, Sid. I forgive everybody. When I'm dead ...."

"Dead!"

"Dead, Sid! It won't be long now. Tell Aunt Polly that I forgive her for hitting me. And please, Sid, will you give my cat to that new girl. Tell her . . . . ."

Sid was already out of the room. He was rushing downstairs, crying "Auntie! Auntie! Tom's dying!"

"Dying?" exclaimed Aunt Polly. She turned as white as a sheet. "Dying? I don't believe it." She rushed upstairs. *Mary,* Tom's cousin, ran after her.

"What's the matter, Tom?" Aunt Polly asked in a trembling voice.

"Oh! Aunt Polly . . . . . ."

"What's the matter, boy?" repeated Aunt Polly.

"Oh! Auntie. It's my toe. It's poisoned!"

"Poisoned! Let me see."

Aunt Polly put her glasses on, and examined Tom's toe. Then she sat down on a chair. She began to laugh and to cry, both together.

"There's nothing the matter with your toe," she said. "Get out of bed! Get ready for school!"

Tom's groans stopped. Then he said, "It's my tooth as well."

"Your tooth? What's the matter with your tooth?"

"It's loose and it hurts badly."

"Open your mouth!"

Tom obeyed.

"Yes," she said. "The tooth is loose. But that won't kill you. Mary, fetch me that strong thread and a lump of hot coal from the fire."

"Oh!" cried Tom, "Don't pull it out. It doesn't hurt now. I can't feel anything. And I want to go to school . . . . . ."

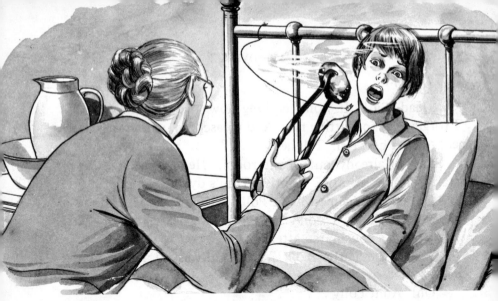

"Ah!" said Aunt Polly, "Now I understand. All this trouble was about school, wasn't it? You want to go fishing, I know. Oh! Tom, why are you like this? I love you but you'll break my heart one day."

Mary came in with the thread and the red-hot coal. Aunt Polly skilfully tied one end of the thread to Tom's tooth. She tied the other end to the bed. Suddenly she pushed the red-hot coal near Tom's face, Tom pulled his head away. The tooth came out!

On his way to school, Tom proudly showed his tooth to the boys. They all thought that Tom was brave. Then Tom met *Huckleberry Finn.*

All the mothers in the village disliked Huckleberry Finn. Indeed he was a very bad example to all boys. He was too lazy to do any work. His clothes were always old and torn and dirty. He never went to school. He slept anywhere. "You mustn't play with Huckleberry Finn!" the mothers said to their sons. "If I catch you playing with Huckleberry Finn, I'll tell your father," they said.

All the boys in the village envied Huck. He never had to wash. He never had to get up early. He could stay up late at night. He could go swimming and fishing whenever he wanted. He never had to go to school. Many boys wished that they were Huck. Tom liked Huck very much.

"Huck! Huck!" Tom called.

"Hullo!"

"What's that?" Tom asked, pointing to something in Huck's hand.

"A dead cat. I'm taking it to the graveyard tonight."

"The graveyard! Tonight!"

"Yes. They're going to dig *Horse Williams* up. He died on Saturday. The doctor wants his body."

"Let me come with you, Huck," Tom begged.

"You can come if you're not afraid."

"I'm not afraid!"

"At midnight then. I'll call for you." Huck used to call for Tom when everybody was asleep. "Me—ow! Me—ow!" he used to call. And Tom used to answer, "Me—ow!"

Tom was late for school, as usual. When he entered the classroom, the teacher called, *"Thomas Sawyer!"*

"Yes, sir."

"You're late again. Why are you late this time?"

Tom was thinking of some excuse. But then he saw the new girl — that lovely girl he had seen in the garden. The desk next to hers was empty. Tom knew that if he made the teacher angry, *Mr. Dobbins* would send him to sit with the girls. Tom decided to be bold.

"I was talking to Huckleberry Finn, sir."

"Talking to Huckleberry Finn! Oh!" exclaimed Mr. Dobbins as if he could not believe his ears.

"Yes, sir. I was talking to Huckleberry Finn," repeated Tom.

Mr. Dobbins picked up his stick. He hit Tom hard, several times. It hurt. But Tom stood there bravely. He did not cry.

"And now," said Mr. Dobbins, "you can go and sit with the girls!"

All the boys laughed at this. Tom walked sadly to the girls' side of the class.

He sat down in the desk next to the new girl's. He was very happy although he was looking so sad.

Tom looked at her. She turned her head away from him. He put an apple on her desk. She pushed it back to him. Tom put it back again. She sat there, looking at it. Then Tom began drawing. After a time, she whispered, "Let me see!" Tom showed her his drawing. "That's nice," she said. "Can you draw a man?" Tom drew a man. "That's very nice," she said. "Can you draw me?" Tom drew her as well as he could. But the result was very funny. "That's lovely!" the girl said. "I wish I could draw."

"I'll teach you," Tom said.

"When?" she whispered.

"After school," he whispered back.

"What's your name?" Tom then asked.

"*Becky Thatcher.* What's yours? Oh! I know. It's Thomas Sawyer."

"That's my name in school. My real name is Tom."

"That's a nice name."

At that moment, a strong hand pulled Tom's ear hard. Mr. Dobbins pulled Tom up by his ear. He led him to his own desk, on the other side of the room. The whole class was laughing loudly. Tom's ear hurt him but he felt very happy.

5

WHAT HAPPENED IN THE GRAVEYARD

It was midnight. Tom was in bed but he was not asleep.
He lay there half-awake and half-asleep. Once he heard a dog
bark, far away. Then he heard the "me—ow" of a cat. Was it
a dream or was it real? "Me—ow! Me—ow!" It was not a
dream! It was Huck. Huck was calling him. Huck was there,
waiting for him. They were going to the graveyard.

Very quickly and very quietly Tom dressed himself. He
climbed out of the window. He walked carefully along the
roof. Now and then, he called "Me—ow! Me—ow!" He
jumped down to the ground. Tom and Huck then started on
their walk to the graveyard.

The graveyard was about half an hour's walk from the
village. It was on a hill in a very lonely spot. Round it was
an old, broken fence. The graves were very, very old.
Wooden crosses marked the graves. The crosses were so old
that they were falling down. Grass was growing everywhere.
When the boys got there, a light wind was blowing through
the trees. The sound of the wind was very sad. Tom was
afraid. He was afraid of the ghosts that were there. And so
was Huckleberry Finn.

The boys made their way in the darkness to HorseWilliams's
grave. There they stood waiting.

"I don't like this place," Tom said.
"Neither do I," Huck said.

"Do you think that Horse Williams is listening?"

"I don't know . . . . Maybe . . . ."

"Oh!" Tom exclaimed suddenly, "Listen!"

"It's the ghosts! They're coming! Oh! Tom, what shall we do?"

"Will they see us?"

"Of course they will. Ghosts can see in the dark, like cats!"

"Sssh! Keep still! Perhaps they won't notice us," Tom whispered.

For a time the two boys stood there silently. Their hearts were beating very fast.

"Look! Look over there!" whispered Tom.

"The ghosts! They're coming for us! They're carrying fire with them! Oh! Tom!"

"Sssh!"

The boys saw three figures moving slowly towards them. One was carrying a lamp.

"They're coming! They've seen us, Tom! They'll eat us alive!"

"Sssh!"

The figures came nearer.

"Tom," whispered Huck, "they're men. That's *Muff Potter's* voice. And there's *Red Joe* with him!"

"Sssh!"

The three men had now reached HorseWilliams's grave. They were only a few feet away from the boys who were behind some trees. They had a small cart with them. In the light of the lamp, the boys were able to see the face of the third man. It was young *Doctor Robinson.* "Here's the grave," the doctor said. "Hurry up! You must finish before the moon rises. Come on, hurry!"

The men started digging. They lifted the coffin out of the grave. Then they broke open the coffin and took out the dead body. They placed it in the cart and covered it.

"There!" Muff Potter said to the doctor. "We've finished. But you must give us five dollars more. If you don't, we'll leave the body here."

"But I've already paid you!" the doctor said.

"Now you must pay us another five dollars," Red Joe said.

"No!" said the doctor, "I shan't give you a single cent more. I've paid you enough already."

"Listen!" said Red Joe. "Pay us that five dollars or you'll be sorry! I know you and I know your father. Your father said that I was a thief and he sent me to prison. I haven't forgotten that. I shall never forget it. Now . . . . . those five dollars!"

The doctor did not answer Red Joe. He simply knocked him down. Then Potter rushed at the doctor. The two men were soon fighting hard. Red Joe jumped up. He picked up Potter's knife which had fallen from his belt. He waited for the right moment to strike. The doctor picked up a board from the grave. With this, he struck Potter a hard blow. Potter fell to the ground. Then Red Joe rushed at the doctor. He struck at him with Potter's knife. The knife went deep

into the doctor's chest. He fell to the ground — dead.

By this time, the moon had risen. The boys saw the terrible fight clearly. Then the moon went behind a cloud and the boys crept away in the darkness. When the moon came out again, Red Joe was standing over the two bodies. He bent down and took some money from the doctor's pocket. He put the knife into Potter's right hand. After a time, Potter moved. He groaned and then he sat up. He looked round him. He saw the doctor's body. Then he saw the knife in his own right hand. He dropped it at once.

"Oh! Joe, what have I done?" he asked in a trembling voice.

"You've killed him, Muff!"

"Killed him? I? But . . . . . !" Muff rubbed his aching head. "I can't remember."

"I just can't remember . . . . We were talking about those five dollars. Then there was a fight . . . . . . Yes, I can remember that . . . . . . Then . . . . . ."

"Then he hit you with a board. You struck him with your knife. He knocked you down, but you killed him, Muff!"

"I was drunk," Potter said. "I didn't know what I was doing . . . . . . You won't tell anybody, will you, Joe? Promise you won't tell. Promise!"

Potter fell on his knees in front of Red Joe. He begged him again, "Promise me, Joe! Promise you won't tell!"

"I won't tell," promised Red Joe.

Muff Potter began crying like a little child.

"Stop that!" cried Red Joe angrily. "Come on! Let's go! Let's get out of here! You go that way. I'll go this!"

Both men ran away from the graveyard, but Potter's knife was still lying at the side of the dead doctor!

6

TOM AND HUCK ARE VERY MUCH AFRAID

Tom and Huck ran like hares back to the village. Both were very frightened. They rushed inside an old barn. They barred the door, and threw themselves down on the floor. They lay there for some time, breathing heavily. When Tom got his breath back, he said, "Oh! Huck, wasn't it terrible! The doctor's dead!"

"Dead! And somebody will have to hang for it!"

"Shall we tell, Huck?"

"Tell! If we do, Red Joe will be after us. He'll kill us as well!"

"Yes . . . . ," Tom's voice trembled as he spoke.

"Let Muff Potter tell," Huck said.

"Yes, you're right. Let Muff tell! We mustn't say anything . . . . . . Huck, we must swear that we won't say anything."

"We must write it down and sign it with our blood!"

Tom took a piece of wood and wrote these words on it:—
"Huck Finn and Tom Sawyer will say nothing. Let them die if they do." Then each boy pricked his thumb and pressed a little blood from it. With this each signed his name. They then dug a hole and buried the piece of wood.

Suddenly they heard a dog howling. "Listen!" Huck said, "That means death. Somebody's going to die soon."

"Do you mean Muff Potter?" Tom asked. Huck did not answer.

The two boys left the barn. They walked towards the dog. They found the dog standing at the side of a sleeping man.

The man was Muff Potter. The dog went on howling. "Muff will die soon," Huck said.

Tom ran home. He climbed into his bedroom through the window. He thought that Sid was asleep. But Sid heard him. The next morning Sid told his aunt that Tom had been out that night.

The next morning when Tom went downstairs, his aunt asked him no questions. She only looked at him sadly and said, "Oh! Tom, what shall I do? You get worse and worse!"

Tom went to school. The teacher was angry with him as usual. Tom felt very sorry for himself. Mr. Dobbins was against him. His aunt was against him. Perhaps Red Joe was after him. Worst of all, Becky would not speak to him. She thought that Tom liked Amy Lawrence better than he liked her. She turned her back on him. Tom felt that his heart was breaking.

7

MUFF POTTER IS SENT TO PRISON

The next day, everybody was talking about the crime in the graveyard. "It was Muff Potter who did it." "Yes, it was Muff Potter." "He left his knife behind." "It must have been Muff," they all said. Somebody had seen Potter washing that morning. That was an unusual thing. "He was washing the blood off his clothes," they said.

Everybody went to the graveyard to look at Horse Williams's grave. There was a crowd there and Red Joe was in the crowd. The Sheriff brought Potter to the grave. The poor fellow was shaking with fear. "I didn't do it!" he cried. "You can't hang me! I didn't do it! I tell you I didn't do it!" Then, when Potter saw Red Joe, he said, "Oh! Joe, you promised not to tell!"

Then Red Joe told the Sheriff his story of the fight. He told him how Potter had killed the doctor. His story was not all true but everybody believed him. Tom and Huck were among the crowd. They were half-hidden because they were afraid of Red Joe. They listened to Red Joe's story but they were so afraid that they said nothing.

"Is this knife yours?" the Sheriff asked.

"Yes, it's mine. But I didn't kill him," Potter repeated.

Muff Potter was taken to prison. For many nights after that, Tom could not sleep. He had terrible dreams. Sometimes he spoke in his sleep. Often he shouted, "Blood! Blood!" "Don't tell!" "Red Joe's coming!" Sid heard all

this and he told Aunt Polly. But Aunt Polly said that everybody was having bad dreams after that terrible crime. She
herself was.

Little by little, Tom forgot about the crime. Sometimes he
went to the prison and spoke to Potter through the small
window. He took him tobacco and some sweets. He felt
very sorry for poor Muff. And so did Huckleberry Finn.

8

NEW MEDICINE FOR TOM

Tom was not feeling well. He could not sleep as well as he used to. He could not eat as much as he used to. He did not want to run away from school. Sometimes he did not want to play. He was troubled and sad. He was worried over Becky. For some time she was absent from school. Perhaps she was very ill. Perhaps she was dying. Tom was filled with sad thoughts about her and about everything.

"The boy is ill," Aunt Polly thought. "I must give him some medicine."

Aunt Polly was fond of all kinds of medicine. She had a lot of books on this subject. Her newest idea was this — when a boy was ill, he must bathe in cold water every day. And so every morning she made Tom stand outside in the yard. Then she threw ice-cold water over him. After that, she wrapped him in a wet sheet and made him lie in bed. Tom did not get better. He got worse. Aunt Polly tried a new idea. She threw hot water over him instead of cold. That did not help Tom either.

At this time, Aunt Polly heard about a new medicine. It was called Pain-killer. It had the taste of fire. All the same, Aunt Polly made Tom drink it. Three spoonfuls after each meal. Tom hated it. When his aunt was not looking, he quickly poured the medicine into a hole in the floor. Tom was busy doing this one day when the cat came in. Tom poured some of the medicine into its mouth. At once it jumped high into the air. It started dancing on its back legs. It rushed about the room, breaking everything in its path.

It ran about as if it were mad. Tom laughed and laughed. It was a long time since he had laughed so heartily. Aunt Polly heard the noise and came rushing in.

"What's the matter?"

Tom could not speak for laughing. At last he pointed and said, "Look! Look at the cat!"

"What's the matter with it?   You've been giving it that medicine!"

"I don't know," said Tom, still laughing.

Aunt Polly saw the bottle of Pain-killer, the spoon, and a saucer. She guessed the truth.

Tom expected his aunt to be angry. To his surprise she was only thoughtful. "It's not a medicine for cats," she said. "Perhaps it's not a good medicine for boys. You needn't take any more of it, Tom." This was good news for Tom. He began to feel better.

He felt better still when Becky came back to school. She had been ill. Now she was quite well, and lovelier than ever. But Becky was still angry with Tom. She was jealous of Amy Lawrence. She would not speak to Tom. She did not even look at him. All the same, Tom felt happy whenever he saw her.

9

TOM BECOMES A PIRATE

Tom was feeling angry. He was angry with his aunt, with his teacher, and with Becky who still refused to speak to him. "I shall run away," he thought. "Yes, I'll run away and be a pirate. When I'm famous and rich, I'll come back. Then perhaps they will all be kinder to me. They'll be afraid of me!" He met his friend Joe Harper. Joe was looking very angry too.

"What's the matter, Joe?"

"My mother whipped me again this morning. She said that I was a wicked boy."

"Why did she say that?"

"She said I had stolen the cream. I didn't even touch it because I don't like cream. But she said I'd stolen it. She wouldn't believe me when I said I hadn't."

"Let's run away, Joe!"

"That's a good idea. They'll all be sorry then."

"Let's ask Huck to come with us!"

Huck liked the idea of running away, and so the three boys collected some food. At night they sailed down the river on a raft. They landed on a little island called Jackson's Island. There they made a camp. They sat in front of a big fire and ate meat and fish and bread. They ate a great deal and felt very happy.

"Ah! This is the life for me," Tom said. "We don't have to go to school. We don't have to wash. We don't have to get up early. We can go to bed as late as we like. We can go swimming and fishing whenever we want to."

"Yes," agreed Joe, "a pirate's life is the best of all. We'll always be free!"

"What other things do pirates do?" Huck asked.

"Well," explained Tom, "pirates sail the seas in a big ship with a black flag on it. That flag frightens everybody. Pirates capture other ships and take a lot of gold from them. They carry this gold to a lonely island, like this one. They bury it there. Nobody knows where the gold is hidden except the pirates."

The boys talked on and on till they grew tired. Then they fell silent. Tom started to think of his Aunt Polly. He began to feel sorry for her. Joe began thinking about his mother. Was she crying because he had not come home? Even Huck began to feel a little sad, but after a time, they all fell asleep.

10

THE SECRET VISIT

The boys woke up late the next morning. They could not find their raft. The river had carried it away during the night. But that did not trouble them. They made a fire, and cooked some meat, fish, and eggs, and ate a big breakfast. After that they went swimming. After swimming, they walked round the island. They went swimming again. They cooked a big lunch. They ate a lot but they did not talk very much. All of them were growing homesick but they did not say so.

They were sitting thoughtfully over their lunch when suddenly they heard a noise. It came from the river and they ran to the bank to look. Far away, near their village, they could see a number of small boats.

"They're looking for somebody," Tom said.

"Yes," Huck said, "when Bill Turner was drowned, they looked for his body for two days. Whom are they looking for now?"

"Why!" exclaimed Tom, "I know. They're looking for us. They think we're drowned!"

This pleased the boys. It made them feel important. Tom thought, "Now Aunt Polly will be sorry. And so will Becky. Perhaps they're crying . . . . . ."

The boys sat there, watching the boats for a long time. When it grew dark, the boats returned to the village. The boys went slowly back to their camp. They cooked some fish and had a meal. They talked about the boats. They talked about home.

"Shall we go home now?" Joe asked.

"No!" said Tom at once. And Huck said, "No!" But in their hearts they all wanted to go home.

That evening, when Joe and Huck were asleep, Tom swam across the river. He reached the village and made his way to his aunt's house. He reached it at about half-past ten. A light was burning in one window. Through the window, Tom could see his aunt, his brother, his cousin Mary, and Joe Harper's mother. They were talking and did not see him. He crept inside the house and hid himself under his aunt's bed.

"Shut the door, Sid!" Aunt Polly said. "The wind will blow the candles out." Sid shut the door. Aunt Polly went on speaking. "Ah!" she said, "Poor, poor Tom! Where is he now?" She began to cry. "He wasn't a bad boy really. I know that I punished him very often. But he was a good boy. He was naughty sometimes, but he was never a bad boy." She was crying loudly while she was speaking. Mrs. Harper was crying too. "My Joe was a good boy," she said. "I had to whip him sometimes, but he was never a bad boy. Perhaps I was too hard . . . . . ."

"Tom wasn't a good boy." Sid said.

"Oh! Sid, how can you say that!" said Aunt Polly. "He was always good to me. Perhaps I punished him too often. I was wrong. I hope the good God will forgive me!" Aunt Polly went on crying.

They were all crying except Sid. Under the bed, Tom was also crying. He wanted to come out and show himself to his aunt. But he stayed there, listening. He was listening while they were talking. Everybody believed that the boys were drowned. The river had carried their raft to the village. Everyone thought that the boys were dead. "The funeral service will be on Sunday," said Aunt Polly.

Mrs. Harper went sadly home. Aunt Polly went to bed. When she was asleep, Tom crept out. He kissed his aunt and then he crept out of the house. He went back to the camp on Jackson's Island. On the way, he was thinking of the funeral service on Sunday. He was making a plan for that day.

11

THE PIRATES ARE HOMESICK!

When Tom reached the camp, his friends were asleep. When they woke up late in the morning, Tom said nothing about his visit to his aunt. All that morning, the boys played, swam, and fished. Then they sat on the river bank. They were all homesick but none would say so. Tom wrote the name "Becky" in the sand with his big toe. He rubbed it out at once. Then he wrote it again. He wanted to see his aunt and Becky. Huck had no home, but he also wanted to go back to the village. At last, Joe said, "I want to go home!"

"Let's go fishing!" Tom said.

"I don't want to go fishing. I want to go home."

"Let's go swimming!"

"I don't want to go swimming. I want to go home."

"You're like a baby," said Tom. "You want to go home and see your mother!"

"Yes," Joe said, "I want to see my mother."

"You want to stay here, don't you, Huck?"

"Y—e—s," answered Huck. Then he said quickly, "No! I want to go back with Joe. It's lonely here. I know it's nice here, but it's lonely," he repeated. "Let's all go back, Tom!"

"No!" Tom said, "I'm staying here. If you want to go, go! But I'm not going with you."

Huck and Joe walked towards the river. They were ready to swim across to the village. Tom shouted to them, "Wait a minute! Wait! I've got something to tell you." He ran to his friends. He told them about his plan for Sunday. They listened to him. They laughed. "That's a good idea!" they said. Then they went back to the camp with Tom.

They had their dinner.   After dinner, Huck took out his pipe and began smoking. Huck was used to smoking. Tom and Joe wanted to try. They were pirates and pirates always smoked.   Huck made pipes for them and gave them some tobacco. Tom and Joe began smoking.

"Why! This is easy," said Tom. "I like smoking."

"So do I," Joe said.

Both boys went on smoking for several minutes. Little by little, their faces became pale. They dropped their pipes.

"I'm not feeling very well," Joe said.

"I feel sick," said Tom.

Both boys rushed to the trees. Huck sat there, waiting for them.   He had to wait a long time. When the boys came back, they looked very weak and ill.

"How are you feeling now?" Huck asked.

"Better," they said, but their voices were weak. Their faces were still very pale. They sat down but they did not say anything more.

Later, Huck said, "I think I'll have a smoke now. What about you two?" Both boys quickly answered, "No! No!"

12

THE STORM

The boys were glad to go to bed that night. They slept well till midnight. Then a fearful storm awakened them. They were sleeping under some trees when the storm began. The lightning flashed across the sky. The thunder roared and rolled. Soon the rain was pouring down like a river. "To the tent!" shouted Tom. But the noise of the storm drowned his shout. He rushed towards the tent. His friends followed him. They were wet through when they got there. They stood there, shivering. The wind grew stronger. Soon it blew the tent away. The boys ran for shelter under a tall tree near the river. They were very much afraid. The noise of the storm was fearful. Tree after tree fell with a crash. Each boy was thinking, "Will the wind blow our tree down? If it does . . . !"

The storm ended at last. The boys crept back to their camp. But now there was no camp. The tent was gone. The ground was covered with broken branches. Everything was wet through. For a long time they could not make a fire because the sticks were so wet. They tried and tried again. At last they succeeded. But they felt tired and ill. How they wished that they were at home again in their own warm beds, comfortable and safe.

The sun came out again and the boys got dry. They sat round their fire but they did not talk much. They did not feel happy. They were thinking of home all the time. They were wishing that they were there. Tom began to talk about his plan for Sunday again. This made them all feel more cheerful. They played a game of "Red Indians" and fought one another till they could fight no more. They felt more and more cheerful. It was their last night on the island. The next day was Sunday and then they would return to the village and home. That was a happy thought for all of them. Huck took out his pipe and began to smoke peacefully. He asked Joe and Tom if they wanted to smoke. Both boys answered, as before, "No! No!"

13

THE FUNERAL SERVICE

In the village, everybody was talking about the boys. Everyone was sad. How sad Aunt Polly was! And Mrs. Harper! And Becky! Every time Becky heard Tom's name, she began to cry.

That Sunday morning, the church bells rang out sadly. The people of the village walked slowly to the church for the funeral service. Aunt Polly was there with Sid and Mary. Mrs. Harper was there with all her family. All of them were wearing black clothes.

The sad service began. Everybody was crying while it was going on. Many women were crying loudly. Then suddenly, the church door opened. People turned round to look. They could not believe their eyes. Tom was walking in! After Tom came Joe. After Joe there was Huck. Were they real? Were they the ghosts of the drowned boys? The singing stopped. The crying stopped. "Oh!" exclaimed everybody.

The boys were not dead. They were alive! How glad everyone was! How happy Aunt Polly was! How happy Mrs. Harper was! They threw their arms round Tom and Joe. They kissed them many, many times. Nobody welcomed Huck till Tom said, "Huck's come back too. Isn't anybody going to kiss Huck?" "I am," Aunt Polly said. And she kissed Huck warmly. Huck's face went very red. He was not used to kindness.

Tom's plan had succeeded. The boys had planned to return to their village for their funeral service. They had

hidden themselves in the village until the service had begun.
Then they had entered the church.

Everyone was kind to the boys. They were given a very big
breakfast. They enjoyed it very much. After breakfast,
Aunt Polly said to Tom, "Why didn't you come back before?
I thought you were dead. Why didn't you come and tell me
you were safe. You don't love me, Tom! If you did, you
wouldn't stay away." "I do love you, Auntie," Tom said.
"I dreamt about you. That shows that I was thinking about
you, doesn't it?"

"Well . . . yes," Aunt Polly answered. Then she asked,
"What did you dream, Tom?" Tom then told her his
"dream."

14

TOM'S "DREAM"

"I dreamt," began Tom, "that you were sitting here with Sid and Mary and Mrs. Harper. It was on Wednesday night, I think. Yes, it was . . . . . ."

"That's right, Tom, go on!"

"There was a wind and it nearly blew the candle out. You said, 'Shut the door, Sid!' And Sid got up and shut the door."

"Why! Tom, that's wonderful. Go on!"

"Then you said, 'Tom wasn't a bad boy really. He was naughty sometimes. But he was never a bad boy.'"

"Yes, I did say that. And then?"

"And then you began to cry. Mrs. Harper began to cry too. And she said that Joe was a good boy really. She was sorry that she had whipped him."

"That's true, Tom. That's all true. I must go and tell Mrs. Harper about this. It's really wonderful."

"Then Sid said that I wasn't a good boy."

"Yes! Yes!"

"And you said, 'How can you say that, Sid? Tom was always good to me. I punished him too often. I was too hard on him.' You were crying all the time."

"That's how it was, Tom. Just like that. Go on!"

"You talked about the raft and the funeral service on Sunday. But you were crying so much that I couldn't hear everything. Mrs. Harper was crying a lot too. Then Mrs. Harper said that she had to go home. You went to bed then."

"So I did, Tom! Well, this is really wonderful. Can you remember anything else? I'll have to tell Mrs. Harper about it."

"When you were asleep, I kissed you."

"Did you really, Tom? Did you really?"

"Really, Aunt Polly."

"You're a good boy, Tom. I always knew that you were a good boy really."

Aunt Polly was very pleased. She looked very happy. She went straight to the cupboard in the kitchen. She looked for the nicest apple there. She gave it to Tom, saying again, "I always knew you were a good boy, Tom."

Sid had listened to Tom's story. At the end of it, he looked very thoughtful. "That's a very strange dream!" he thought to himself.

15

TOM IS IN TROUBLE

After his adventure on Jackson's Island, Tom was a hero to the other boys. They all admired him, and they envied him as well. Tom and Joe told their adventures to the boys a hundred times. The boys thought that Tom and Joe were great men. And so did the girls.

Becky wanted very much to speak to Tom. But Tom was very proud now. He pretended to like Amy Lawrence more. Poor Becky was very sad. When Tom saw that, he was pleased. One day, when Tom was talking to Mary Austin, Becky said to Mary, "Oh! Mary, will you come to my party? Mother has said that I can invite all my friends." While Becky was saying this, she was looking at Tom. She was hoping that Tom would ask to come. But Tom paid no attention to Becky. He turned round and began talking to Amy. All the boys and girls wanted to go to Becky's party — all but Tom and Amy. Poor Becky was so sad that she cried. But after a time, she dried her eyes and smiled. She had thought of a plan.

Becky sat down near *Alfred Temple*. They began to look at a picture-book together. They both laughed loudly over the pictures. Tom heard them laughing. At once he was jealous. Suddenly he did not want to talk to Amy any more. She seemed to him quite stupid. He left her and went home. How he hated that Alfred Temple with his fine clothes.

When Tom had gone, Becky lost all interest in the book — and in poor Alfred. She did not want to look at another picture. She jumped up and shouted to Alfred, "Go away! I hate you!" At first Alfred could not believe his ears. Then he understood everything. He had never liked Tom. Now he hated him. He hated him and he wanted to hurt him. How? What could he do?

Alfred went into the classroom. He saw Tom's spelling-book on his desk. He opened it at the page for the next lesson. Then he poured ink all over that page! "There!" he said to himself, "That will teach you, Thomas Sawyer. Mr. Dobbins will whip you. And I shall be glad!" While Alfred was doing this, Becky looked in through the window. She kept quiet, thinking, "I hate Tom Sawyer. I shall always hate him. Always till I die! Let Mr. Dobbins beat him! I'll be glad if he does."

Tom found more trouble waiting for him when he got home. Aunt Polly was very angry.

"What's the matter, Auntie?"

"That dream . . . . . . I told Mrs. Harper about it. But it wasn't a dream. And you knew that it wasn't, Tom. Joe had told her that you were really here that night. Now Mrs. Harper thinks I'm an old fool. I know she does. It's all your fault!"

Poor Aunt Polly began to cry. Tom felt very sorry, and ashamed as well.

"It wasn't a dream, Auntie. That's true. I really did come that night. But I came to tell you that I wasn't dead. I didn't want you to worry. I'm very sorry, Auntie!"

"Is that the truth, Tom?"

"It is!   Oh, It is!"

"And did you really kiss me, Tom?"

"Yes, I did — because I do love you, Aunt Polly."

Aunt Polly began to look happy again.

16

MORE TROUBLE FOR TOM

Tom felt happier after this talk with his aunt. He went back to school quite cheerfully. On the way, he met Becky. "Becky," he said, "I'm sorry about this morning. I hope you're not angry with me." Becky looked at him very coldly, "Don't talk to me, Mr. Thomas Sawyer," she said. "I'm never going to speak to you again!" Tom was very angry. He answered her angrily. Becky thought to herself, 'You wait till the spelling lesson. Mr. Dobbins will beat you when he sees your book.'

Then Becky herself got into trouble. Mr. Dobbins kept a book in his desk. When the class was working, he used to take it out and study it. Nobody in the class knew what that book was. But everyone was eager to know. Mr. Dobbins always locked his desk and so no one had seen the book. But that afternoon, when Becky was passing the desk, she saw that the key was in the lock. She was alone in the classroom. Quickly she opened the desk. Quickly she took out the book and looked at it. The book was called "Modern Medicine". While she was looking at it, someone came into the classroom. She looked up. There stood Tom Sawyer! She closed the book so quickly that she tore a page. She was afraid, ashamed, and angry. She began to cry. "You'll tell Mr. Dobbins! I know you will. And he'll whip me! Oh! I hate you, Tom Sawyer! I hate you!" Becky ran blindly out of the classroom.

"What is the matter with her?" Tom asked himself.

"I shan't tell. But Mr. Dobbins is sure to find out. Then he'll punish her. I'll be glad then!"

The spelling lesson began. The pupils took out their books. Mr. Dobbins quickly noticed the ink on Tom's book. "I didn't do it!" Tom cried. "It isn't my fault!" The master paid no attention. He beat Tom in front of the class. Becky felt very sorry then. "Shall I tell Mr. Dobbins about Alfred?" she asked herself. But then she thought, "No, I shan't. I know that Tom will tell about me and Mr. Dobbins' book. So I shan't tell about Alfred and the ink!"

When the class was working quietly, Mr. Dobbins took out his book. He began to read. Becky was watching him. She was waiting fearfully for him to find the page that she had torn. Tom was watching Becky. "Poor Becky!" he thought. "How frightened she is!" He forgot his anger against her. The master turned over a page or two. Then he looked up angrily and shouted to the class, "Who did this?" He showed the torn page to his pupils. Nobody said a word. Everybody trembled in his seat.

"Joseph Harper, did you tear my book?"

"No, sir!"

"Benjamin Rogers, did you?"

"No, sir!"

"Alfred Temple, did you?"

"I? Oh, no sir."

When Mr. Dobbins had asked all the boys, he began to ask the girls.

"Amy Lawrence, did you tear my book?"

"No, sir!"

"Gracie Miller, did you?"

"No, sir!"

Mr. Dobbins came to Becky.

"Rebecca Thatcher, did you tear it?"

Becky's face was as white as a sheet. She was trembling all over. She could not lift her head to answer the master. She looked guilty. Mr. Dobbins clearly believed she was. At that moment Tom stood up and said, "Sir, I did it! I tore your book. It wasn't Becky!"

"Come here, Thomas Sawyer!" Mr. Dobbins said. Tom walked out to the front of the class. He looked at Becky when he was passing her desk. Her eyes were shining and she looked happy. "She likes me now," thought Tom, and felt happy too. Mr. Dobbins hit Tom hard, many times. That did not trouble Tom. While the master was hitting him, he was thinking, "Becky likes me now!" When Mr. Dobbins had finished, he said, "You'll stay in after school for two hours!" That also did not trouble Tom. "Becky will wait for me. I know she will," he thought happily.

Becky was indeed waiting for him when he came out of school. She said, "Tom, you're wonderful! You're the nicest boy in the world. How noble you are, Tom!"

17

PRIZE DAY

It was nearly the end of the term. The examinations were near. Mr. Dobbins was making the boys work very hard. If they didn't work, he beat them. Nearly every lesson, some boy was beaten. The boys were getting angry about this. One day they all met together and made a plan. What was their plan? It was this: Mr. Dobbins had no hair. He always wore a wig. The boys planned to paint his head a golden colour. The painter's son promised to do this. Mr. Dobbins was living in his house. The boy could do the painting while Mr. Dobbins was asleep in his chair after his lunch. "You can be sure," he said to the class, "that Mr. Dobbins will have a golden head on Prize Day."

Prize Day came. All the pupils sat quietly in the school hall. They were dressed in their best clothes. Their faces looked very clean. Their hair was carefully brushed. Their parents were sitting there too. All the people of the village were there. First of all, different boys and girls recited poems. Tom did too. He stood on the platform in front of everybody, shouting:
"Let me be free!
Let me die if I can't be free!
Freedom! Give me freedom!"
He stopped suddenly. He had forgotten the words. He looked round helplessly. He saw Mr. Dobbins' face, red with anger. He simply could not remember another word of his poem. He looked very foolish standing there. He felt very foolish. He rushed off the platform, his face bright red with shame.

After the recitations, Mr. Dobbins stood up. He went to the blackboard. He began to draw a map of America. He was going to ask his pupils some questions on the geography of America. While he was drawing, the fun began. A cat suddenly appeared above his head. It was hanging from a piece of string. A boy in the room above was holding the string. The cat could not make any sound because its mouth was closed with a tight bandage. Slowly the cat came down. It came nearer and nearer to the master's head. Soon it was near enough to touch the master's wig. It pulled it off! Then the cat was quickly pulled up. Everybody was looking at Mr. Dobbins' head. The painter's son had done his work well. Mr. Dobbins' head was a bright, golden colour. It shone like the sun. His pupils laughed loudly. Their parents laughed loudly. Everybody roared with laughter — except poor Mr. Dobbins.

18

THE TRIAL OF MUFF POTTER

After Prize Day came the long Summer holidays. Tom and all the boys of the village were free. Free to go swimming. Free to go fishing. Free to do what they liked! All the same, Tom was feeling worried. Muff Potter's trial was coming near. Should Tom tell what he had seen in the graveyard? Or should he keep quiet? He was frightened of Red Joe. And so was Huck.

Potter had been in prison for some time. People had stopped talking about him. Now they began talking again. "He's guilty. Of course he's guilty. His knife was there. He must be guilty." Everybody thought that Muff had killed the doctor — everybody but Tom and Huck — and Red Joe of course.

One day, Tom had a talk with Huck.

"Have you told anybody about Red Joe?" Tom asked.

"Told anybody! Why! If we open our mouths, Red Joe will kill us too."

"Yes, he will, that's true."

"Everybody is against Potter." Tom went on. "I feel sorry for him."

"And so do I," said Huck.

"Potter isn't a bad fellow. It's true that he used to drink a lot. When he was drunk, he didn't know what he was doing. But he isn't a bad fellow," repeated Tom.

"You're right, Tom."

"I wish we could do something to help him, Huck . . . . "

"So do I. But if we tell, Red Joe'll be after us . . . . . ."

The two boys often went to the prison where Potter was. They had long talks with him through the little window. They gave him tobacco and sweets. Just before his trial, Muff thanked the boys with tears in his eyes. "You've been true friends to me," he said. "I'll never forget how good you've been to me."

These words of Potter made Tom feel very sad and ashamed. He could not sleep. He had terrible dreams. Once more, he began to talk and to scream in his sleep. Tom went to the Court on the first day of the trial. He came home sadder than ever. Everybody believed Red Joe. It was certain that Potter must hang. Tom felt that this must not happen. Secretly, he went to Muff's lawyer and told him the true story of the crime.

Then came the last day of the trial. The Court was crowded. Poor Muff stood there as white as a sheet. He looked like a man in a dream. Red Joe was there too, of course. Several men spoke against Potter. "I found Potter's knife beside the doctor," said one. "I saw Potter washing the blood off his clothes," said another. Then Red Joe told his story. Everyone believed him. Everyone believed that Muff had killed the doctor. Everyone was waiting for the judge to say that Potter must hang for his crime.

A voice was heard, "Call Thomas Sawyer!" it said. People looked at one another in great surprise. Tom Sawyer? What did he know about the crime? Tom stood up. He looked round the Court. He was afraid. Everybody was looking at him. Everybody was waiting eagerly for him to speak. He was too frightened to say one word. "Don't be afraid, my boy," the judge said kindly. "You're safe here. Tell us what you know." Then a lawyer began to ask Tom many questions:

"Is your name Thomas Sawyer?"

"Yes, sir."

"Where were you on the night of June the seventeenth?"

Tom saw Red Joe's face. He could hardly speak. Then he said bravely, "I was in the graveyard, sir."

"Speak up!" said the lawyer. "You needn't be afraid."

"I was in the graveyard, sir," repeated Tom in a louder voice.

"Were you near Horse Williams's grave?"

"Yes, sir."

"How near?"

"As near as I am to you now."

"Were you hiding?"

"Yes, sir."

"Where?"

"Behind some trees near the grave."

Tom was speaking in a loud voice now. Red Joe was looking at him.

"Were you alone in the graveyard?"

"No, sir. I was there with . . . . . a friend."

"Tell us what you saw, my boy."

There was deep silence in the Court. Tom told the true story of the crime. He ended with, "Red Joe did it, sir. It was Red Joe who killed the doctor. It wasn't Muff!"

Red Joe jumped up. He rushed to the nearest window. Some men tried to hold him back. He knocked them down. He jumped out of the window into the street below and began running. Many people rushed after him. It was too late. Red Joe had got away.

Everybody praised Tom. Everyone thought that he was a brave boy. But Tom and Huck were afraid. They were afraid that Red Joe would come back and kill them. They stopped going out after dark. Many nights Tom could not sleep. His bad dreams came back. But, little by little, as time passed, Tom forgot his fears. Red Joe did not come back to the village. Perhaps he would never come back again.

19

TOM AND HUCK DIG FOR TREASURE

Tom was fond of books about pirates. He liked reading books about buried treasure. One day he said to Huck, "Let's go and dig for treasure!" "Dig for treasure!" exclaimed Huck. "Where? Where do pirates bury their treasure?"

"Pirates always bury their treasure in haunted houses or under certain trees," explained Tom.

"But don't they come back and get it?"

"Well, yes. Sometimes they do, but usually they don't. They die or they go to prison or somebody kills them. The treasure stays there till somebody finds it. I'm sure we can find some treasure if we look in the right place . . . . . ."

"Where's the right place?"

"You know that dead tree at the top of the hill, Huck? I'm sure that there's some treasure buried under it. Let's try there first of all!"

So Tom and Huck set out to dig for treasure. The tree was about three miles away. The day was hot and the hill was steep. The boys were carrying spades with them. They were hot and tired when they reached the tree. They began digging. After an hour, they sat down for a rest. Then they began digging again. They dug and they dug. But they found nothing. At last Tom said, "Huck, I've made a mistake. We've been digging in the wrong place. We must come back at midnight. Then we must find where the shadow of the tree falls. The right place is at the end of that shadow. If we dig there, we shall find something. I'm sure, Huck!"

At midnight, the two boys were back again at that tree. They began to dig at the end of the shadow. They dug and they dug. Again they found nothing.

"We must try somewhere else," Tom said.

"Where?"

Tom had an idea. He pointed to an old house not far away, "There," he said, "in that haunted house over there. That's the place for treasure!"

"Oh, no, Tom. Not there!" cried Huck. "I don't like haunted houses. I'm afraid of ghosts!"

"We'll go there in the day-time. There won't be any ghosts then. Ghosts only walk about at night. Besides, Huck, nobody has seen any ghosts in that house. I don't think that there are any."

"Are you sure, Tom?"

"Quite sure."

"Then I'll come with you — if you go in the day-time!"

The two boys walked down the hill. They passed the haunted house. They stood still for a moment, looking at it. The house was a sad sight in the moonlight. The fences were all broken. The roof had fallen in. The garden was full of tall grass. Suddenly the boys felt afraid. They began to run. They did not stop running till they reached the village!

20

THE HAUNTED HOUSE

The next day at twelve o'clock, the boys were back again in the haunted house. They had brought their spades with them. They were ready to start digging. Suddenly Tom remembered.

"Oh! Huck, I forgot. We can't do any digging today."

"Why not?"

"It's Friday. We can't go inside a haunted house on a Friday. It brings bad luck!"

The two boys went home. But the next day, at the same time, they were there again. They carried their spades inside the house, and then left them in a corner while they looked round the place. The house was very silent and the boys felt a little afraid.

"I don't like this place," whispered Huck.

"Neither do I," whispered Tom. "But perhaps we'll find something here. This is the right place for treasure. Come on, let's have a look!"

They looked round the rooms downstairs. They found no signs of treasure.

"Let's try upstairs," Tom said in a whisper. And the boys crept softly up the stairs. They went slowly and carefully, for the stairs were very old. Although the stairs were dangerous, the boys arrived safely at the top. Then they began looking around. Suddenly they heard a noise. They jumped. Footsteps! Somebody was coming. The boys looked for somewhere to hide. But there was no hiding-place. They stood there, shaking with fear. Their hearts were beating fast. Who was coming. A ghost? Ghosts? Pirates? Robbers? Red Joe? Tom looked at Huck. Huck looked at Tom. Their faces were white. They did not speak. They lay on the floor and looked down, through the cracks, to the room below.

Two men came in. One of them was well known to the boys. People called him the *Spaniard.* He was a stranger in the town. He had long white hair and he wore dark glasses. He begged in the streets. People gave him money because he was dumb and almost blind. The other man was unknown to the boys. The two men sat down and began to talk. Both men were talking.

"Why! The Spaniard isn't dumb!" exclaimed Huck.

"Sssh!"

Then they heard the Spaniard say, "I don't like this place. I tell you it's dangerous." The voice was the voice of Red Joe. The Spaniard was really Red Joe. The two boys could hardly breathe from fear.

"I'm not staying here long," Red Joe went on. "This place is too dangerous for me. There are one or two things that I have to do. After that I'll be glad to get away from here. You go back up the river. Wait for me. Then we'll go on to Texas together."

The two men were speaking in low voices. It was hard for the boys to hear what they said. But they heard Red Joe say more than once, "I'm not leaving here till I've done one or two important jobs." The boys thought, "He means to kill us before he goes!" At last Red Joe said, "I'm tired. I'm going to sleep. You must stay awake and watch." Red Joe went to sleep. The other man stayed awake for a time. Then his head dropped. Soon he too was asleep.

"Come on, Huck," whispered Tom. "Now's our chance. Let's go!" Tom stood up. He took a step forward. The boards under him gave a loud crack. He stood still. "Wait!" Both boys lay there, in great fear, waiting.

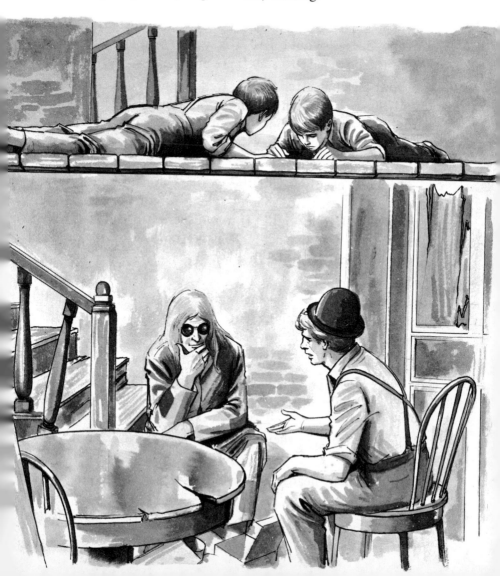

21

RED JOE AND HIS TREASURE

The sun set and the boys were still waiting. It was fast growing dark. Would Red Joe wake up before morning? Would the boys have to stay there all night?

About an hour after sunset, Red Joe woke up. He looked round him. He saw his companion asleep. He kicked him hard. "Come on," he said. "We must get out of here at once." "We must hide the money before we go. We can't carry it about with us."

The boys clearly heard the words "money" and "hide". Their eyes began to shine. They forgot to feel afraid! Treasure! "I told you!" Tom whispered to Huck. "We've come to the right place!" The two boys watched the men through the cracks in the floor.

The two men lifted up a heavy stone. Red Joe took out his knife and began digging a hole. He went on digging till his knife struck something hard.

"What's that?"

"Wait a minute!" And Joe went on digging.

"It's a box. Help me to pull it out!"

Red Joe and his companion pulled up the box. They broke it open.

"Gold! Gold!" they cried in joy. They were both very excited.

Above their heads, the two boys were trembling with excitement.

The two men pushed their hands into the coins. "Gold! Gold!" they cried again and again.

"Murrel's men used to come here," Red Joe's companion said. "It's theirs."

"And now it's ours," said Red Joe.

"Where shall we hide it?"

"Let's bury it somewhere?" Red Joe said. "But we need a spade." He looked round him, searching for a spade. His eyes fell on the spades that the boys had left there. "How did those spades get here?" he asked. He walked towards them. He picked them up and examined them.

"There's fresh earth on them! Somebody's been here lately . . . . . . No, we won't bury the money here. It isn't safe. We'll take it to my place."

"Number One or Number Two?" asked his companion.

"Number Two. Under the Cross. That's the safest place."

"Yes, that's safe," agreed the other. "Let's go now. I don't feel safe here."

"Neither do I," Red Joe said. "But before I go, I want to know something. I'd like to know who brought those spades here. I'm not going till I've found out!"

The boys, who were listening, began to shake with fear.

"It was those boys. Those two boys we saw yesterday."

"Ah, yes! Those!" Red Joe laughed wickedly. Then he went on, "They may be here today. Perhaps they're hiding. I'm going upstairs to see . . . . . ."

The boys' hearts almost stopped beating.

Red Joe began to climb the stairs. The boys heard his heavy footsteps. Nearer and nearer they came. "He'll kill us, that's certain," they were thinking. They grew so frightened that they could not think. They simply lay there, waiting for death. The footsteps were very near now. The boys almost stopped breathing.

Crash! A stair broke under Red Joe. He fell to the floor. He was soon on his feet again.

"Come on!" said the other man. "You'll break your neck if you go up those stairs again. Come on. Let's get out of here. I tell you I don't like this place!"

"Neither do I," said Red Joe, rubbing his leg.

The two men went away, carrying the treasure with them. The boys climbed down the stairs and rushed away. When they were near the village, they stopped. Tom asked Huck, "They've taken the treasure to Number Two. Where's Number Two, Huck?"

"I don't know. We'll have to find out." Then he asked, "Tom, what did Red Joe mean when he said he had something to do before he left? Is he going to kill us, Tom?"

"How do I know?" said Tom. "I'm going home."

22

TOM AND HUCK GO AFTER RED JOE'S TREASURE

Tom could not sleep that night. He could not sleep at all. After breakfast, he went to look for Huck.

"Huck," Tom said, "we must find out where Red Joe is. We must get that treasure."

"Yes, I've been thinking about it. Number Two is the place. But where's Number Two?"

"I don't know . . . . . . Perhaps it's the number of a house . . . . . ."

"But houses haven't any numbers here."

"That's true . . . . . . Do you think it's the number of a room? A room in the inn, maybe?"

"That's it! It's the number of a room."

"We can easily find out. There are only two inns in the village."

"Let's go and look now. I'll go."

"No, Huck! You wait here for me. I'll go. I shan't be long."

After about half an hour, Tom came back.

"Red Joe isn't in Number Two at Hopkins' Inn," he said. There's a young clerk staying there. He's been staying there for the last three years. He's a nice fellow. I know him. I think Red Joe is at Miller's place. *Fred Miller* says that Number Two there is a very strange room. Nobody goes in and nobody comes out. But somebody's there. Somebody who likes to drink. Fred has heard somebody singing, somebody drunk . . . . . ."

"Red Joe drinks a lot," Huck said.

"Listen, Huck! I've got a plan. The back door of that room is in a side street. If we can get a key, we can get inside. You get all the old keys you can. I'll do the same. We're sure to get one that fits the lock. Then, one night, when there's no moon, we'll open the door. We'll see what's inside. Perhaps we'll find the treasure there, Huck!"

The next moonless night, the boys crept into that side street. Tom's pockets were full of old keys. Like a thief, he made his way to the back door of Number Two. Huck waited for him at the end of the street. He waited for a very long time. He began to feel very worried. Had Red Joe killed his friend? He did not know what to think. He did not know what to do. Suddenly, like a flash of lightning, Tom was rushing past him. "Run!" he shouted. And Huck ran!

The boys ran to an old barn at the end of the village. Tom was breathless. For a time he could not speak. Then he said, "Oh! Huck, it was terrible. I tried all the keys but I couldn't find one that opened the door. Then I turned the knob. The door opened. It wasn't locked, you see. I went in and . . . . . oh!"

"Go on, Tom! What happened then?"

"I trod on Red Joe's hand!"

"What?"

"Yes, Huck. He was lying on the floor. It was dark and I couldn't see. I trod on his hand, Huck!"

"Did he see you? Did he wake up?"

"Oh, no! I think he was drunk . . . . . ."

"If he's still asleep, then we can get the treasure," Huck said.

"I'm not going back there again. You go if you like. But I'm not going there while Red Joe's there!"

"We'll have to watch. When Red Joe goes out, you can go in and get the box."

"That's it, Huck! You watch every night. When Red Joe goes out, come and call for me. I'll come out when I hear you. But I'm not going in while he's there — not for all the treasure in the world!"

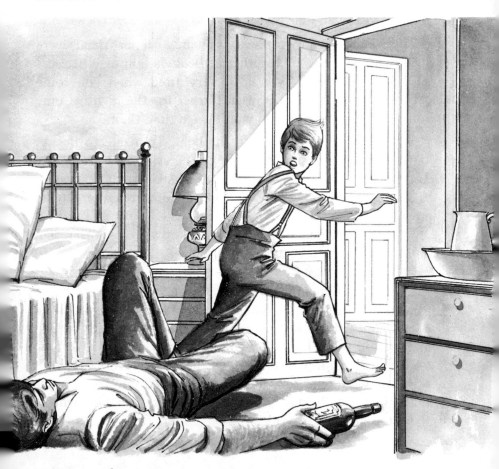

23

BECKY'S PICNIC

For several nights after this, Tom did not sleep well. He was waiting for Huck's "me—ow". But Huck did not call him. Then Becky Thatcher came back from her holiday in the city. Tom and Becky played happily together. Tom almost forgot about Red Joe and his treasure.

Then came the day of Becky's picnic. All her friends were invited. They all met together at Becky's house. "Becky," said *Mrs. Thatcher*, "you'll be very tired when you come back tonight. Stay with Susan Harper for the night. Come home in the morning. You won't be so tired then."

While they were walking to the boat, Tom said to Becky, "Don't stay at Susan Harper's. Stay at *Widow Douglas's*. You know how nice she is. And she makes such nice cakes. I'll stay there too. Then we can go home together in the morning."

"Well," answered Becky, "I don't know . . . . . What will mother say? She'll be angry with me!"

"She won't know," Tom said.

Then Tom remembered Huck. "I ought to go back home tonight," he thought. "Perhaps Huck will come for me. If he comes, and if I am not home, he won't know where to find me." But then Tom thought, "He may not call for me tonight. He didn't last night or the night before. I don't think he will come tonight." Tom decided not to go home that night. "I'll stay at Widow Douglas's. Becky will be there too. It'll be very nice."

The boat sailed down the river with Becky and all her friends on board. They went far down the river. They landed near a wood. It was a very hot day but the wood was full of shade. It was cool there. The children played games until lunch-time. They sat down under the trees. All of them were hungry. They all ate a lot.

After lunch, they went to visit a big cave. This was an adventure for the children. The cave was dark and cold inside. The children carried candles to light their way. They went this way and that, along different passages. But they did not go far because they were afraid of getting lost. They spent a long time in the cave. The cave was a most exciting place. They came out, laughing and singing. All of them were excited and happy. When night was falling, they all got back into the boat. Singing and laughing, they returned to the village. What a happy day!

24

HUCK SAVES THE LIFE OF WIDOW DOUGLAS

That night Huck was hiding in that side street behind the inn. At eleven o'clock, all the lights in the inn went out. "Everybody's asleep now," thought Huck. "I'm going to sleep too." At that moment, he heard a faint sound from the inn. Somebody had closed a door softly. Somebody was coming very quietly down the street. Huck quickly returned to his hiding-place.

Two men passed by. One of them was carrying a heavy box. "That's the treasure," Huck thought. "They're taking it away. They're going to hide it somewhere else. I'll have to follow them. There's no time to tell Tom. I'll have to follow them by myself." The two men walked for a time beside the river. Then they turned and walked up the hill. Huck followed them all the way. It was a moonless night and that helped Huck.

The men came to Widow Douglas's house. They stopped. Huck stopped. He was quite near the men and could hear every word they spoke.

"There are lights in three rooms. Somebody must be there with her," Red Joe said angrily.

"You can't do anything tonight," the other man said. "Come on! Let's go! Leave her alone. Forget it!"

"Forget it!" exclaimed Red Joe. "Never! I'll never forget it! Her husband sent me to prison. When I came out, I came here to kill him. But he'd died before I got here. It doesn't

matter. She'll have to pay instead of him. I'm going to kill her tonight!"

"There's somebody there!"

Red Joe was not listening. He went on, "Perhaps I shan't kill her. No! I'll do something worse. I'll cut her face and I'll cut her ears. She'll look very pretty when I've finished with her. That'll punish her!" He turned to his companion, "You've got to help me. If you don't, I'll kill you too."

"Hurry up then! What are you waiting for?" the other man said.

"I'm waiting till the lights go out."

After these terrible words, the two men were silent. They stood there, waiting for the lights to go out.

Huck was very frightened. He crept away very quietly. Then he began to run. He ran fast till he came to a house.

This was the house of *Mr. Jones,* a brave and honest old man. There Huck stopped. He knocked at the door. "Let me in! Please! Please let me in!" he cried.

"What's the matter?" the old man called from his bedroom window. Then he came downstairs with his two strong sons. All three stood there in the doorway.

"Why! It's Huckleberry Finn." the old man said.

"Please let me in!" Huck begged. "Something terrible is going to happen!"

"Come in! Come in, and tell us!"

Huck went inside and told his story.

Two minutes later, Mr. Jones and his two strong sons were running towards Widow Douglas's house. Each of them was carrying a gun. Huck did not go with them. He hid himself and he waited. Suddenly he heard a shot. They were shooting. Huck jumped up from his hiding-place. He ran away as fast as he could.

25

HUCK FINDS HIMSELF AMONG FRIENDS

Very early the next morning, Huck was again knocking at Mr. Jones's door. "Come in, my boy! Come in!" the old man said, very kindly. "You're a brave fellow, Huck. You'll always be welcome here. Come in and have some breakfast with us!" Huck sat down at the table but he could not eat anything. "You look ill, Huck," said Mr. Jones. "Drink this cup of tea!" Then the old man told Huck what had happened that night. "We weren't able to catch them," he said, "but one of them was wounded. He can't be far away. We've told the men in the village. They're going to search the woods for those criminals. Can you tell me what they looked like?" "Well," said Huck slowly, "one of them is that Spaniard. You've seen him about the village. He has got long white hair and he's dumb. The other fellow is a stranger. He's tall and thin and he's wearing old clothes."

"I know them both," Mr. Jones said. Then he asked, "What made you follow them?" "Well, ... I couldn't sleep. I went out for a walk. I saw those two. One of them was carrying a heavy box. 'He's stolen something,' I thought, 'I'll follow him.' They went towards the river. Then they turned right and went up the path that leads to Widow Douglas's place. I was close behind them all the time. I could hear almost every word they said. When they reached Widow Douglas's, they stopped. They began talking. I heard that Spaniard say, 'I'll cut her face and I'll cut off her ears.' And then . . . . . ."

"But isn't that Spaniard dumb?" asked Mr. Jones.

"Oh! No, he isn't! He's . . . . . ." Huck suddenly stopped. He was telling the old man too much. He did not want to get into more trouble. He had had enough.

"Who is he?" the old man asked. "Tell me, my boy! Don't be afraid! We're your friends and you can trust us." He spoke so kindly that Huck answered, "He's Red Joe!"

"Red Joe!" The old man nearly jumped off his chair in his excitement.

"Red Joe!" he repeated. He could not believe his ears.

"Yes, Red Joe!"

"Are you sure?"

"Yes, I recognised his voice."

"Well!" the old man could find no words to say what he thought. His sons had stopped eating. They were looking at Huck with their mouths wide open. Their eyes were as big and round as saucers.

"Ah!" said the old man at last. "Now I understand . . . ."

At that moment, Widow Douglas came in. She came to ask for news about the robbers. She wanted to know what had happened to them. Mr. Jones and his sons told her the story. When they had finished, Widow Douglas was trembling with fear and excitement. "How can I thank you?" she asked, with tears in her eyes. "You saved my life!" "You mustn't thank me," the old man said. "It wasn't me. It was . . . . . ." He stopped. He wanted to say, "It was Huck who saved you from Red Joe." But he had promised Huck to keep Huck's name out of the story. He did not want Huck to get into more trouble.

26

TOM AND BECKY ARE LOST

It was a lovely Sunday morning. Nearly everyone in the village went to church. When the service was over, they came out of church. They stood in little groups round the church door, talking to one another in a friendly way. Mrs. Thatcher went up to Mrs. Harper. "Thank you," she said, "for looking after Becky last night. It was kind of you to let her stay at your house."

"Becky! At my house!" Mrs. Harper exclaimed in great surprise.

"Didn't she stay at your house last night?" asked Mrs. Thatcher, suddenly much afraid.

"Oh, no!"

Mrs. Thatcher felt suddenly very ill. Her face went pale. Her legs began to tremble. She had to sit down.

Aunt Polly came up to them. "Tom hasn't come home yet," she said. "I feel so worried. I'm afraid that he has run away again. Did he sleep at your house last night, Mrs. Harper?"

"No, he didn't."

Aunt Polly turned to Joe Harper. "Do you know where Tom is?" she asked.

"No, I don't. He came on the picnic with all of us . . . . . ."

"Was he on the boat coming back?"

Joe thought for a time. Then he answered. "No, ... I didn't see him on the boat coming back."

Aunt Polly asked many boys. Nobody had seen Tom or Becky on the boat as they came back.

"Oh! They're lost in that cave!" screamed Aunt Polly.

Everybody said that the children had lost their way in the cave. All the men in the village at once got ready to look for the two children. Soon there were two hundred men on the road. Judge Thatcher, who was Becky's father, led the men to the cave. Then the search began.

The women stayed in the village, waiting. They were very frightened. All that night they waited, but no news came. In the morning a message reached them from Judge Thatcher. "Send more candles, rope, and food!" That was all. That message made Mrs. Thatcher very ill. It nearly broke Aunt Polly's heart.

Widow Douglas went again to Mr. Jones's house. Huck was there in bed. He was very ill and had a high temperature. The village doctor was in the cave and so Widow Douglas looked after Huck. She nursed him carefully. She looked after him like a mother.

Late that day, more news came. The men had not found the children. But they found the names "TOM" and "BECKY" on a rock. The children had written their names with the smoke from their candles.

For three days and three nights, the search went on. In vain! The children were not found. Everyone in the village lost hope. "They are dead," the people thought. Mrs. Thatcher was very ill. Aunt Polly waited and prayed.

27

TOM AND BECKY IN THE CAVE

Tom and Becky walked about the cave with the other boys and girls. They played and laughed and sang together. Tom and Becky, however, walked much deeper into the cave and soon left the others far behind. They came to a small stream. Here they stopped for a time to rest and to look round. Tom saw a passage that looked very interesting. "Let's go along this way. Let's explore!" Tom said to Becky. They walked into the passage. Soon they were deep inside the cave. Now and then Tom made marks on the wall. "They will show us the way back," he said. Then suddenly a great number of bats flew out. They rushed blindly at the children. One flew at her candle and put it out. Tom tried to beat the bats away but more and more came. Both children began running as fast as they could. When the bats had stopped following them, the children stopped running. They were breathless and afraid. They sat down to rest.

It was very silent there. The silence and the darkness frightened Becky. "Let's go back now, Tom," she said. "Can you find the way?" "Of course I can. But we must go back by a different way. Don't let us go where those bats are!"

The children walked on and on. They lost their way. Tom knew that they were lost but he said nothing. Becky began to cry. "Oh, Tom!" she said, "We'll never find the way out. Never!" But Tom answered,"We shall,Becky. I know we shall!"

The children walked on and on. They sat down for a time. Then Tom blew Becky's candle out. "We can see well enough with one candle," he said. After a time, there was only one candle left. What would they do when that was finished? After a rest, the children began walking again. They reached a small stream and sat down beside it. They drank. Tom had a piece of cake in his pocket. He gave half of it to Becky and kept the other half for himself. But he ate only a little of his half. The rest he put in his pocket for Becky. "Becky," he said, very quietly, "this is our last candle. We'll have to stay here. Here there's water for us to drink . . . . . ."

"They'll come and look for us, won't they, Tom?"

"Of course they will! Perhaps they're looking for us now . . . . . ." Tom suddenly fell silent. Mrs. Thatcher thought that Becky was at the Harpers'. Both remembered this. They sat there in silence. Then their last candle went out. All was dark then. There was no light anywhere. Deep night was all around them. Becky began to cry. She cried and cried. Then she fell asleep. Tom slept too. When they awoke, they ate the rest of Tom's cake. That was very little. Both of them were very hungry, very tired, and very sad.

Suddenly they heard shouts. "Becky! Becky! They've found us!" Tom shouted. Both children jumped up. They shouted as loudly as they could. They ran in the direction of the shouting. But they could not move fast in the darkness. And they were too weak to shout loudly. The shouts stopped. Soon there was silence again.

Sadly the children returned to their places near the water. They fell asleep. When they awoke, they were hungrier than ever. Becky was so weak that she could hardly stand up. She was too tired to cry. But Tom said, "I'm going to try again." He took some string from his pocket. He tied one end of the string to a rock. Then, with the string in his hand, he walked along a passage. That passage ended in a big rock. Tom went back. "Well, I must try another one," Tom said to himself. Tom tried another passage. Then another. Then another. "Whatever happens, I must keep on trying," he thought.

At the end of the next passage, something very strange happened. Suddenly, there was a light. Tom saw a man's hand, holding a candle. The figure of a man appeared. Tom's heart beat fast. Help had come at last, he thought joyfully. Then, in the light of the candle, Tom saw who that man was. It was Red Joe. Tom was so frightened that he could not move. He waited for Red Joe to come and kill him. But Red Joe did not stop to see who the boy was. He rushed away.

After a time, Tom went back to Becky. He was trembling like a leaf. But he said nothing to Becky about Red Joe.

Becky was growing weaker and weaker. Tom went on trying passage after passage. He had no hope of finding the way out. But he continued saying to himself, "I must keep on trying!"

28

SAVED!

The village was very sad. Three days had passed. For three days and three nights, the men had searched the cave − in vain. No hope was left. Mrs. Thatcher thought she was dying. Aunt Polly was still waiting, but there was little hope in her heart. Then, at midnight, all this was changed. The church bells rang out merrily. Everybody heard them. Everybody rushed into the street. "Tom and Becky are safe! They've been found! They're home again!"

Yes, the two children were riding through the streets in an open carriage. Everyone was shouting with joy. Nobody could think of sleeping any more that night. The carriage took the children to Judge Thatcher's house. All the village gathered there. There was Aunt Polly − whose face was shining like the sun. "Thank God! Thank God!" she kept on saying. Mrs. Thatcher felt suddenly better again. Tom had to tell his story a great many times. He was the hero of the hour.

"We were very hungry," he said. "I had to do something. Poor Becky! She was so tired. And so I took my string and went along another passage. At the end of it, there was daylight. Yes, daylight! Well, I couldn't believe it. But I ran towards it. There was a hole in the rock and the daylight was coming through. I pushed my head through that hole. There was the river shining below me. Oh! How happy I was! I ran back to Becky. I brought her to the hole. We climbed through it. We were outside. Out of that cave! How happy we were! We sat there till we saw two men in a boat. We waved and they came to us. They gave us something to eat and drink. Then they brought us here. And here we are!" Tom ended joyfully.

Afterwards Tom went to see Huck who was still sick in bed. He was still staying with old Mr. Jones. Widow Douglas was still looking after him. She was beginning to like Huck as if he were her son. The two boys had a long talk together.

"Red Joe's friend is dead," Huck told Tom. "They found him in the river."

"Drowned?"

"They say that Red Joe killed him and then threw him into the river."

"Red Joe!"

That name still made the boys tremble. Their fear of Red Joe would end only when Red Joe was dead. He did die soon afterwards. His death was a terrible one. It happened like this:

Tom met Judge Thatcher one day. The Judge, who liked Tom, spoke to him in a very friendly way. "Nobody will get lost in that cave again," he said. "I've closed the cave with an iron door."

When Tom heard that, his face turned white. "You've closed the cave!" he cried.

"Oh, sir, Red Joe's inside!"

"Red Joe!" exclaimed the Judge. Without saying anything more, he went to the cave with his men. The Judge opened the door. There, near the door, lay Red Joe – dead! His knife was beside him. He had tried to cut a hole in the iron door with his knife. In the end he had died of hunger. They buried him just outside the cave.

29

RED JOE'S TREASURE

Tom and Huck were not sorry about Red Joe. They had always been afraid of him. Now their fear was gone. Now they could think about Red Joe's treasure.

"It's not in that room in the inn," Huck said. "I've looked there."

"The treasure's in the cave," Tom said. "And I'm going to get it. Will you come with me, Huck?"

"Of course I will. I'm not ill now."

"Then we'll go this afternoon," Tom said. "We'll need our spades, some string, some bags, candles and matches . . . . oh, and plenty of things to eat!"

That afternoon, the two boys went down the river in a small boat. Tom showed Huck the hole in the rock. It was the hole through which he had escaped with Becky. Tom and Huck climbed through the hole. They lit their candles and walked along a narrow passage. Tom was leading the way. Suddenly he stopped. He held up his candle and pointed. "Look, Huck!" he said, "There's the Cross. 'Number Two, under the Cross,' Red Joe said. Well, here's the Cross. The money must be here, Huck. This must be the place!"

"I don't like it here, Tom," Huck said. "Let's go, Tom! Red Joe's ghost will come after us if we stay. Let's go!"

"No, Huck. I'm not going till I've found that treasure. Come on, Huck! I'm sure it's here."

Tom led the way farther down the passage. The boys reached a big rock. There Tom stopped and pointed. "Look,

Huck! Footprints! And a match-stick! Somebody struck a match here. Somebody lighted a candle . . . . . . I'm going to dig under that rock."

The two boys started digging. Suddenly their spades struck something hard. A box! "The treasure!" Tom cried. They pulled the box up. They broke it open. It was full of gold coins. "Gold!" shouted the boys. They looked at each other, full of joy and excitement. "Gold!" they shouted again. Then, like two madmen, they began to laugh and sing and dance.

"We're rich, Tom!"

"We're rich, Huck!"

The box was too heavy for the boys to carry, so they filled their bags with the gold coins. They carried them carefully to their boat. They rowed back to the village in triumph! They borrowed a cart from Mr. Jones and put their bags on it. They did not tell him what was inside.

"Mrs. Douglas is waiting for you, boys," Mr. Jones told them. "She's giving a party and she wants you to be there. Come on! She's invited me as well. We can all go together." Then Mr. Jones, Tom, and Huck and their cart all went to Widow Douglas's.

30

WIDOW DOUGLAS GIVES A PARTY

The boys left the cart, with the treasure on it, outside the house. They went inside. All the important people of the village were there. Widow Douglas kissed the boys when they came in. When she saw how dirty they were, she said, "Go upstairs and have a good wash! We won't begin till you're ready."

When the boys were upstairs, Huck said to Tom, "I'm not going down with all those people there. Let's jump out of the window, Tom! Let's run away while we can!"

At that moment, Sid came in. He looked at the boys' dirty clothes and he asked, "Where have you been? Aunt Polly has been looking for you all the afternoon." Tom did not answer. He went on washing his hands. Then he asked, "Why is Widow Douglas giving a party like this?"

"It's for Mr. Jones. He saved her that night when Red Joe was here. And he has a surprise for everybody. But it won't be a surprise because everybody knows already."

"Knows what?" Tom asked.

"Knows that Huck followed Red Joe and then went to fetch Mr. Jones."

"Who told them?" asked Huck.

"Sid did," Tom said and he kicked Sid hard. "You love

telling tales, don't you? Now go and tell Aunt Polly that I kicked you!"

Sid ran downstairs. The two boys followed him slowly.

"Come on, Huck! It'll soon be over," Tom whispered.

Downstairs they found a crowd of people. There was a lot of talking. Then Mr. Jones stood up to speak. Everybody became silent. Mr. Jones told them all about Huck. He told them how Huck had saved Mrs. Douglas from Red Joe. Everybody looked at Huck and clapped. Huck felt miserable. "When can we get away from here?" he whispered to Tom.

Mrs. Douglas went up to Huck. "Huck," she said, "you saved my life. Come and live with me. I'll try to be a mother to you. I'll look after you like a mother. I'll send you to school. Later on, I'll find some work for you. I haven't much money, Huck, but you shall have a half of it. You shall never be poor and miserable again."

"Huck isn't poor!" Tom cried. "He's rich!" Everybody looked at Tom in great surprise. Tom went on, "You don't believe me? Well, I'll show you!"

Tom went out and came back, carrying a heavy bag. He poured the gold coins out on the table for everyone to see. Everyone looked but they could hardly believe what they saw. Then Tom brought the other bags in and emptied them. "Half of it is Huck's and half of it is mine," Tom explained.

For some time, nobody said anything. They were all too surprised to speak. At last they asked, "Where did you find all that gold, Tom. Tell us!" Tom told the story of Red Joe's treasure. "Well! Well!" was all they could say. They were too surprised to say more.

31

A HAPPY ENDING

Everyone in the village was excited over Red Joe's treasure. Many people began digging to find treasure for themselves. But they never found anything. Tom and Huck were now rich. Judge Thatcher put their money into a bank where it would be safe. Judge Thatcher liked Tom more and more. He took a special interest in the boy. "What a brave boy he is!" he thought. "He saved Becky in the cave. He found Red Joe. I think that one day he will be a great soldier. Certainly I shall always help him."

Yes, Tom's life was a happy one now. But Huck was growing more and more unhappy. He did not like his new life. He felt very sorry for himself. Mrs. Douglas was very kind to him. But Huck did not like her kindness. She made him go to bed early. He had to eat with a knife and fork. He had to meet a lot of people. Worst of all, he had to go to school. After three weeks, Huck ran away where nobody could find him.

It was Tom who found him at last. Tom found Huck in an old barn. He was lying on some sacks and smoking his pipe. He was very dirty – and very happy. "Huck," Tom said, "you must come home. You can't live in a place like this. You're a rich boy now. Besides, Widow Douglas is so sad."

"I can't go back there, Tom. I hate that life. I have to wear clean clothes. I have to wash myself every day. I have to comb my hair. She won't let me smoke. She won't let me go out at night. She makes me go to school!"

"You must come back, Huck," Tom repeated.

"No, Tom! I like my old life best. I'll never go back!"

"Listen, Huck! All boys have to wear clean clothes and to wash and to go to school. We all have to, Huck!"

"I'm not like other boys," Huck said. "Their life isn't for me. I must be free. I must do what I like. I can't breathe in that house . . . . . ."

"I'm very sorry about that, Huck. It's a great pity. You see, Huck, I'm collecting a new band of men. We're going to attack people. We're going to steal from the rich and give to the poor. Like Robin Hood, Huck! But I can't have any rough fellows in the band. The band is only for quiet fellows who go to school — fellows who know something. I don't want anybody to say, 'Tom Sawyer's band is a rough crowd.' And so, Huck, you won't be able to join the band. It's a great pity, Huck!"

Huck looked very disappointed. "Let me join, Tom!" he begged.

"I can't, Huck. I'd like to, but I can't. If you come back home, you can join. But you must go to school, like the rest of us."

Huck was silent. He thought for a long time, then said, "Well, I'll try again, Tom. I'll come back home. Promise that you'll let me join if I come back!"

"I swear!"

"I'll try again," repeated Huck. "I shan't be in the house all the time. I'll be able to smoke if I'm with the band. Tell me, who's going to be Robin Hood, Tom?"

Questions and discussion points

Chapter 1

Let's talk

Find the true sentence. Why is it true? Why are the other sentences not true?

(a) Tom often got into trouble.
(b) Tom had not been swimming that afternoon.
(c) Tom was not as strong as the boy he had a fight with.

Let's write

1   Copy these sentences and fill in each space with a name from the story.

    (a) Tom _____ lived with his Aunt _____ because his mother had died.
    (b) Tom had a brother called _____ .
    (c) Instead of going to school, Tom played 'Cowboys and Indians' in the woods with his friend _____
        _____.

2   Which of these can you find in the picture facing page 1?

brooch   cane   glasses   jug

kettle   necklace   stick   stool

Copy the ones you have found. There are four.

3   How did Aunt Polly find out that Tom had been swimming
    that afternoon? You may copy a sentence from the story to
    help with your answer.

4   Copy and finish these sentences.

    (a) Aunt Polly sewed Tom's collar together so that _____
         _____ .

    (b) Tom and the new boy started fighting when _____
         _____ .

    (c) Aunt Polly guessed Tom had been fighting again
         because _____ .

Chapter 2

Let's talk

Find the true sentence. Why is it true? Why are the other
sentences not true?

(a) Tom fetched some water from the village pump.
(b) Tom didn't let Ben do any whitewashing.
(c) Tom didn't do much work that day.

Let's write

1   Copy each question with the correct answer from the box.

    (a) What was in the bucket Tom was carrying?
    (b) What did Aunt Polly hit Jim with?

(c) What did Tom eat?

> Her shoe.   Whitewash.   Ben's apple.

2   Copy this list of words and underline the odd one out.

> broken toys   marbles   an orange   pieces of string

Why is it the odd one out?

3   Tom discovered two important laws. Copy them and fill each space correctly with a word from the box.

(a) If a man must do something hard, then that _____ work. If he likes to do something hard, then that _____ work.

(b) If we _____ get something, we want it badly. If we _____ get something easily, we do not want it.

> can   cannot   is   isn't

4   Look at the picture on page 8. You can see Tom Sawyer and some of his friends. Think about these questions.

Is Tom working hard? What is he doing? What are his friends doing? Do you think Tom is clever?

Now write a heading 'Whitewashing the fence' and underneath write three sentences about what happened.

Chapter 3

Let's talk

Find the true sentence. Why is it true? Why are the other sentences not true?

(a) Tom got on well with his brother Sid.
(b) Tom liked the girl who lived at the new boy's house.
(c) Tom knocked the sugar basin off the table.

Let's write

1 Write these sentences in the order in which they happened.

- Somebody threw a lot of water on Tom's head.
- A girl threw a rose over the fence to Tom.
- Tom finished the whitewashing.
- Aunt Polly hit Tom.
- Tom went for a walk.

2 Choose the correct word from the brackets to complete each sentence. Write the whole sentence.

(a) The boys (divided, parted, shared) themselves into two armies.
(b) Tom had (burgled, robbed, stolen) some sugar from his aunt's cupboard.
(c) Aunt Polly came running into the room when she (heard, listened, noticed) the crash.

3   Choose the best title for the paragraph on page 10
     beginning 'On his way home, . . .'.

     (a) Amy Lawrence
     (b) The beautiful girl
     (c) The rose

     Copy the one you choose.

4   Here is the answer to a question:

                 Because he was a bad boy.

     The question begins 'Why . . .?'. Now write the question
     and then copy the answer underneath.

Chapter 4

Let's talk

Find the true sentence. Why is it true? Why are the other
sentences not true?

     (a) Tom had a poisoned toe.
     (b) Tom was a friend of Huckleberry Finn.
     (c) Becky Thatcher didn't pay any attention to Tom.

Let's write

1 Match the beginnings of these sentences with the correct endings.

(a) Tom pretended to be ill,   because he made the teacher angry.

(b) Aunt Polly pulled Tom's tooth out   to play with Huckleberry Finn.

(c) None of the mothers in the village wanted their children   when he started drawing.

(d) Tom had to sit with the girls   because he didn't want to go to school.

(e) Becky took an interest in Tom   with a piece of thread and a red-hot coal.

2 Copy and finish these sentences.

(a) Tom groaned loudly so that _____ .
(b) The boys in the village envied Huckleberry Finn because _____ .
(c) Mr. Dobbins took Tom back to his own desk when

_____ .

3 Skim through the chapter and find words that mean nearly the same as:

(a) looked carefully at
(b) shaking
(c) asked

Write the words in order, to match (a), (b) and (c) above.

4 Write a heading 'Huckleberry Finn'. Which of these words
   describe him?

> dirty   hard-working   lazy
>
> polite   uneducated   well-behaved

(a) Copy the ones you choose.
(b) Now write three sentences about Huck. The words you
     have chosen will help you.

Chapter 5

Let's talk

Find the true sentence. Why is it true? Why are the other
sentences not true?

(a) The graveyard was near the village.
(b) Dr. Robinson paid the diggers another five dollars after
     they had dug up the coffin.
(c) Red Joe killed Dr. Robinson.

Let's write

1 Copy this paragraph and fill each space with a word from
   the box.

At midnight, Tom went to the _____ with Huckleberry
Finn. Both _____ were very frightened. They saw
three men go to Horse Williams' _____ . Then Red

Joe and Muff Potter dug up the _____ . Dr. Robinson told them _____ to do. When the diggers had put the dead body into the _____ , they asked Dr. Robinson for more _____ . He refused to give them _____ . There was a _____ and the doctor was killed.

boys	cart	coffin	fight	grave
graveyard	money	more	what	

2   Copy and complete each question and answer correctly with words from the box.

   (a) _____ did Huck call Tom? By sounding like a
       _____ .

   (b) _____ did the boys hide? Behind some _____ .

   (c) _____ did Red Joe take from the doctor's pocket?
       Some _____ .

Where	How	What
cat	money	trees

3   Copy these words and underline the spelling mistake.

   groaned   knocked   reached   started   wispered

   Can you write the correct spelling too?

4   Write a heading 'The fight' and think about these questions.

Who started the fight? What was the fight about? How did
the doctor attack Muff Potter? How was the doctor killed?
Who killed him? What did Muff Potter think had happened?

Now write four sentences about what happened.

Chapter 6

Let's talk

Find the true sentence. Why is it true? Why are the other
sentences not true?

(a) Tom and Huck decided not to tell anyone about what they
     had seen.
(b) Muff Potter was asleep in the barn.
(c) Aunt Polly didn't know that Tom had been out all night.

Let's write

1   Write these sentences in the order in which they happened.
     ● They heard a dog howling.
     ● Tom felt very sorry for himself.
     ● Tom and Huck ran back to the village.
     ● They swore they wouldn't say anything.
     ● They rushed inside an old barn.

2   Tom and Huck swore they wouldn't say anything about what

they had seen. Copy this paragraph and fill in the missing words from the story. (Don't look back at the chapter yet!)

Tom took a piece of _____ and wrote these_____ on it: "Huck Finn and Tom Sawyer will say nothing. Let them _____ if they do." Then each boy pricked his _____ and pressed a little _____ from it. With this each signed his _____ . They then dug a _____ and buried the piece of _____ .

Now look back to page 23 to check your work.

3   Copy and complete this list of reasons why Tom felt sorry for himself.

   (a) His aunt _____ .
   (b) The teacher _____ .
   (c) _____ might be after him.
   (d) Becky _____ .

4   Unjumble the letters of these words.

   (a) givelal
   (b) squonties
   (c) yeodombs

   Write the words in order, to match (a), (b) and (c) above.

Chapter 7

Let's talk

Find the true sentence. Why is it true? Why are the other sentences not true?

(a) Muff Potter confessed that he had killed the doctor.
(b) Red Joe made Tom and Huck feel frightened.
(c) Nobody visited Muff Potter in prison.

Let's write

1   Tom was sleeping badly. Copy and complete these sentences about what he did.

> i)He _____ .
> ii)_____ in his sleep.

What words did he shout?

> iii)" _____ "
> iv)" _____ "
> v)" _____ "

What did his brother do about this?

> vi) Sid _____ .

2   Write these words in alphabetical order.

> doctor   blood   prison   crowd   knife

3 Copy these sentences and fill each space with 'was' or 'wasn't' so that the sentence is true for the story.

   (a) "He _____ washing the blood off his clothes," they said.
   (b) His story _____ true but everybody believed him.
   (c) Everybody _____ having bad dreams after that terrible crime.

4 Choose the best title for the paragraph beginning 'The next day . . . ' on page 25.

   (a) The murderer
   (b) The graveyard
   (c) Rumours

Copy the one you choose.

Chapter 8

Let's talk

Find the true sentence. Why is it true? Why are the other sentences not true?

(a) Aunt Polly's medicines didn't work.
(b) Aunt Polly gave Tom the cat's medicine.
(c) Aunt Polly said that Tom must finish all the medicine.

Let's write

1   How do you know that Tom was not feeling well? Copy
    and complete this list of his symptoms.

     i)_____ sleep.
     ii)He _____ .
     iii)_____ from school.
     iv)Sometimes _____ play.

2   Copy these questions with the correct answers from the box.
    (a) What was the new medicine called?
    (b) Who did Tom give it to?
    (c) Who was still angry with Tom?

    ┌───┐
    │ The cat.   Becky.   Pain-killer.   │
    └───┘

3   Copy and complete each sentence with a word from the
    box.

    (a) Front is the opposite of _____ .
    (b) Mad is the opposite of _____ .
    (c) Laughing is the opposite of _____ .

    ┌─────────────────────────────────┐
    │ crying   sane   back   │
    └─────────────────────────────────┘

4   Write a heading 'Aunt Polly's treatment' and think about
    these questions.

    What was the newest treatment? What did Tom have to
    do? Did he get better? How did Aunt Polly change the

treatment? Did it work? Would you like to have Aunt Polly's treatment?

Now write four sentences about the treatment.

Chapter 9

Let's talk

Find the true sentence. Why is it true? Why are the other sentences not true?
(a) Tom and Becky had become good friends.
(b) Tom and his friends took a boat to Jackson's Island.
(c) Tom and his friends had second thoughts about staying on the island.

Let's write

1   There are five reasons why Tom liked being on the island — three are negative and two are positive. Copy and complete this table.

Positive	*Negative*
i)_____ bed _____ .	i)We don't _____ .
ii)_____ whenever we want to.	ii)_____ wash.
	iii)_____ early.

2   Copy and finish these sentences.

    (a) Tom decided to run away because _____ .
    (b) Joe Harper was angry because _____ .
    (c) The boys liked a pirate's life because _____ .

3   Skim through the chapter and find a word or phrase that means nearly the same as:

    (a) beat
    (b) take possession of
    (c) stopped talking

    Write the words or phrases in order, to match (a), (b) and (c) above.

4   Which of these phrases do you associate with pirates?

        a lot of gold   black flag   camp fire
        stolen cream   lonely island

    (a) Copy the ones you choose.
    (b) Write a heading 'A pirate's life' and underneath write three sentences about what it is like. The words you have chosen will help you.

Chapter 10

Let's talk

Find the true sentence. Why is it true? Why are the other

sentences not true?

(a) The three boys didn't think about their homes while they were on the island.
(b) Tom made a secret visit to his home.
(c) Sid was very unhappy about his missing brother.

Let's write

1 Match the beginnings of these sentences with the correct endings.

   (a) People in small boats were looking for   for Sunday.

   (b) The three boys really wanted   under his aunt's bed.

   (c) Tom hid   Tom and his friends.

   (d) Everybody believed that   to go home.

   (e) Tom's funeral was planned   the boys were drowned.

2 Copy this list of words and underline the odd one out according to the story.

   eggs   fish   fruit   meat

   Why is it the odd one out?

3 Choose the correct word from the brackets to complete each sentence. Write the whole sentence.

   (a) The boys could not find (their, there, they're) raft the next morning.

(b) Tom (arrived, came, reached) Aunt Polly's house at about half past ten.

(c) They were all crying (accept, except, exception) Sid.

4 Here is the answer to a question:

Because they thought the boys had drowned.

The question begins 'Why . . .?'. Now write the question and then copy the answer underneath.

Chapter 11

Let's talk

Find the true sentence. Why is it true? Why are the other sentences not true?

(a) The boys didn't really want to stay on the island.
(b) Huck had made a special plan for Sunday.
(c) Tom and Joe enjoyed smoking.

Let's write

1 Copy these questions with the correct answer from the box.

(a) Who wrote the name 'Becky' in the sand with his big toe?
(b) Who wanted to see his mother again?

(c) Who made pipes for his two friends?

> Huck. Tom. Joe.

2 Write down the reasons why the boys wanted to go back to the village.

- They were homesick.
- They wanted to go to school.
- It was lonely on the island.
- They didn't like making their own meals.
- They wanted to see their families and friends again.

3 Skim through the chapter and find the words that tell you how people said things and then copy and complete this list.

a------d   r------d   s-----d
a---d   s--d

4 Write a heading 'Smoking' and think about these questions.

How did Tom and Joe feel when they smoked for the first time? What were they smoking? What did they do?

Now write two or three sentences about what happened.

Chapter 12

Let's talk

Find the true sentence. Why is it true? Why are the other sentences not true?

(a) The storm started as soon as they had gone to sleep.
(b) The three boys sheltered in their tent.
(c) They were going to go back to the village on Sunday.

Let's write

1   Copy this paragraph and fill each space with a word from the box.

The boys were woken by a terrible _____ . There was _____ and lightning and the _____ was very strong. It blew their _____ away, so they had to shelter under a tall _____ . Many other _____ were blown down. The _____ got very wet. When the storm ended, they found their _____ had gone and everything was wet through.

boys	camp	storm	tent
tree	trees	wind	thunder

2   The storm was very loud so Huck and Joe couldn't hear what Tom said. Copy the sentence from page 36 that gives

this information.

3   Which of these can you find in the picture on page 37?

> braces   feather   fire   raft
> rain   shoes   stick   tent

Write down the ones you have found. There are four.

4   Choose the best title for the paragraph beginning 'The sun
     came out . . . ' on page 37.

(a) Red Indians
(b) After the storm
(c) Round the camp fire

Copy the one you choose.

Chapter 13

Let's talk

Find the true sentence. Why is it true? Why are the other
sentences not true?

(a) Everyone was surprised when Tom and his friends walked
     into the church.
(b) Everyone was pleased to see Huck again.
(c) Everyone wanted to punish the boys.

Let's write

1   Copy and complete each question and answer correctly with
    words from the box.

    (a) _____ was the funeral service? On _____
    morning.

    (b) _____ did Aunt Polly wear to the funeral?
    _____ clothes.

    (c) _____ did the boys hide themselves until the service
    began? In the _____ .

What	Where	When
Black	village	Sunday

2   Write these words in alphabetical order.

    funeral   village   breakfast   church   ghosts

3   Copy these sentences and complete them with a word from
    the box.

    (a) Kindness is the opposite of _____ .
    (b) Succeeded is the opposite of _____ .
    (c) Entered is the opposite of _____ .

left	cruelty	failed

4   Copy and finish these sentences.

    (a) _____ while the service was going on.

(b) _____ because they were so happy.
(c) _____ because he wasn't used to kindness.

Chapter 14

Let's talk

Find the true sentence. Why is it true? Why are the other sentences not true?

(a) Tom told Mrs. Harper about his "dream".
(b) Aunt Polly believed everything that Tom said.
(c) Sid believed everything that Tom said.

Let's write

1   Look at the picture on page 40 and copy and complete these sentences.

    (a) Aunt _____ is sitting in a chair. She is an
        _____ lady. She wears _____ to help her to see.
    (b) _____ is telling his aunt about his _____ .
        He is standing _____ his aunt's chair.
    (c) _____ 's brother _____ is listening too, and so
        is the little girl called _____ .

2   On page 40 Tom says:

        "There was a wind and it nearly blew the candle out."

This means:

(a) The wind was near the candle.
(b) The candle wasn't blown out.
(c) The candle was blown out.

Copy the one you choose.

3   Copy these sentences and fill each space with 'was' or 'wasn't' so that they are true for the story.

(a) 'Tom _____ naughty sometimes. But he _____ never a bad boy.'
(b) Mrs. Harper _____ sorry that she had whipped Joe.
(c) Then Sid said that Tom _____ a good boy.

4   Write a heading 'The nicest apple' and think about these questions.

Where did Aunt Polly find the apple? Why did she give it to Tom? Do you think he deserved it?

Now write two or three sentences to explain what happened.

Chapter 15

Let's talk

Find the true sentence. Why is it true? Why are the other sentences not true?

(a) After his adventure, Tom was unpopular with the other

children.
(b) Becky saw Alfred pouring ink over Tom's spelling book.
(c) Aunt Polly was very pleased to see Tom when he got home.

Let's write

1 Write these sentences in the order in which they happened.

- Becky looked at a picture-book with Alfred Temple.
- Tom had an adventure on Jackson's Island.
- Tom got into trouble when he went home.
- The other children admired Tom.
- Alfred poured ink on to Tom's spelling-book.
- Becky invited the other boys and girls to her party.

2 (a) Skim through the chapter to find the word that means 'somebody who has done something very brave'.
(b) In this story, who was that person?
(c) How did the other boys and girls react to him?

3 Copy these words and underline the spelling mistake.

adventure   classroom   interest   truoble

Can you write the correct spelling too?

4 Here is the answer to a question:

Because Mrs. Harper thought she was a silly old fool.

The question begins 'Why . . . ?'. Now write the question and then copy the answer underneath.

Chapter 16

Let's talk

Find the true sentence. Why is it true? Why are the other sentences not true?

(a) Tom tore Mr. Dobbins's book.
(b) Tom didn't know who had torn Mr. Dobbins's book.
(c) Tom took the blame for tearing Mr. Dobbins's book.

Let's write

1   Copy these sentences and fill each space with a name from the story.

   (a) Mr. ＿＿＿＿ kept a book called " ＿＿＿＿
       ＿＿＿＿ "in his desk.
   (b) ＿＿＿＿ came into the classroom while ＿＿＿＿
       was looking at Mr. ＿＿＿＿ 's book. ＿＿＿＿ tore
       a page of the book.
   (c) ＿＿＿＿ told Mr. ＿＿＿＿ that he had torn the
       book so that ＿＿＿＿ would not be beaten.

2   Copy and complete these sentences.

   There were three reasons why Becky found out about
   Mr. Dobbins's book:
       i)The key ＿＿＿＿ .
       ii)＿＿＿＿ alone ＿＿＿＿ .
       iii)Like everyone else, she ＿＿＿＿ .

3   Choose the correct word from the brackets to complete
    each sentence. Copy the whole sentence.
    (a) Mr. Dobbins quickly (noticed, punished, marked) the
        ink on Tom's book.
    (b) Becky was (awaiting, expecting, waiting) for
        Mr. Dobbins to find the page she had torn.
    (c) Becky could not lift her head to (answer, reply, say)
        the master.

4   Write a heading 'Tom's trouble' and think about these
    questions.

    How many times was Tom beaten in front of the class?
    Did he deserve to be beaten? Why did he take the blame
    for something he hadn't done? Would you take the blame
    for something somebody else had done?

    Now write three or four sentences to explain what
    happened. You can give your own views too.

Chapter 17

Let's talk

Find the true sentence. Why is it true? Why are the other
sentences not true?

(a) Mr. Dobbins was unpopular with the schoolboys.
(b) Tom recited a whole poem very well.
(c) Mr. Dobbins's hair had been painted gold.

Let's write

1 Match the beginnings of these sentences with the correct endings.

    (a) The examinations were held — when they saw Mr. Dobbins's head.

    (b) The pupils were dressed in their best clothes — by a cat.

    (c) Tom was very embarrassed — at the end of term.

    (d) Mr. Dobbins's wig was pulled off — because he couldn't remember his poem.

    (e) Everybody laughed — on Prize Day.

2 Unjumble the letters of these words.

    (a) garyn
    (b) fralptom
    (c) hudlage

Write the words in order, to match (a), (b) and (c) above.

3 Copy this paragraph and fill each space with an appropriate word from the story.

Prize Day was held at the end of _____ . All the people from the _____ were there. The boys and girls recited _____ . Tom forgot the _____ of his _____ . He felt very _____ and rushed off the platform. The schoolmaster, Mr. Dobbins, decided to test the pupils' _____ . While he was doing this, his _____ was pulled off by a _____ and everybody laughed.

4   Write a heading 'Mr. Dobbins' and think about these
     questions.

     What did he look like? Where did he live? Was he a bad
     teacher? What happened on Prize Day? Why did
     everybody laugh?
     Write three or four sentences about what happened.

Chapter 18

Let's talk

Find the true sentence. Why is it true? Why are the other
sentences not true?

(a) Nobody believed that Muff Potter had killed the doctor.
(b) Tom was very nervous when he gave evidence.
(c) Red Joe was captured in the street.

Let's write

1   Copy these sentences and fill the spaces with names from
     the story.
     (a) The trial of _____   _____ was held during the
         long summer holidays.
     (b) _____ and _____ knew the truth about what
         happened in the graveyard.
     (c) _____   _____ jumped out of the courtroom
         window and ran away.

2   Copy these questions with the correct answers from the box.

(a) Who visited Muff Potter while he was in prison?
(b) Who spoke kindly to Tom during his trial?
(c) Who had killed the doctor?

> Red Joe.   Tom and Huck.   The judge.

3   Copy and finish these sentences.

(a) _____ because they were frightened of Red Joe.
(b) _____ when he had to give evidence.
(c) _____ as soon as he heard what Tom said.

4   Write a heading 'The trial of Muff Potter' and think about these questions.

Why was Muff on trial? What would be the punishment if he was guilty? How was Muff feeling on the last day of the trial? How did Tom help him? What did Red Joe do? Was Muff guilty?

Now write four or five sentences about what happened.

Chapter 19

Let's talk

Find the true sentence. Why is it true? Why are the other sentences not true?
(a) Huck enjoyed reading books about pirates.

(b) Tom and Huck found some treasure where the shadow of the tree fell.

(c) The haunted house made Tom and Huck feel afraid.

Let's write

1 Copy this paragraph and fill in the spaces with words from the box.

Tom _____ to dig for buried treasure. He _____ Huck about his plan. Huck _____ to go with him. On a hot day, they _____ to dig under a tree. They _____ nothing. Then Tom _____ they must find where the shadow of the tree _____ at midnight. They _____ anything. Then they _____ there would be treasure in the haunted house. But the two boys _____ frightened, so they _____ to go there during the day-time.

agreed	decided	didn't find	fell
found	said	started	thought	told
were	wanted		

2 Here is the answer to a question:

'In haunted houses or under certain trees.'

The question begins 'Why . . .?'. Now write the question and then copy the answer underneath.

3 How do you know that Tom and Huck were afraid of the haunted house? Write the answer in your own words. (You

may also copy one sentence from the chapter.)

4   Which of these things can you find in the picture on
     page 56?

              chimney   fence   ghost   pirate
              rake   roof   spade   treasure

Write down the ones you have found. There are four.

Chapter 20

Let's talk

Find the true sentence. Why is it true? Why are the other
sentences not true?

(a) Tom and Huck started digging for treasure on Friday.
(b) Red Joe was disguised as a Spaniard.
(c) Tom and Huck went to sleep while they were watching the
     two men downstairs.

Let's write

1   Copy these sentences and fill each space with the correct
     word from the box.

     (a) _____ Red Joe has done one or two important
         things, he will be glad to get away.
     (b) _____ the stairs were dangerous, the boys arrived
         safely at the top.

(c) The two boys were frightened ＿＿＿＿＿ the 'Spaniard'
was really Red Joe.

> Although   because   After

2   Skim through the chapter and find words that mean nearly
the same as:

(a) unable to see
(b) unable to speak
(c) asked for money

Write the words and phrases in order, to match (a), (b)
and (c) above.

3   Write the answers to these questions in your own words.

(a) Why were Tom and Huck able to see Red Joe and his
companion?
(b) How might Red Joe know that the two boys were there?
(c) How did Tom and Huck feel about what they saw and
what they heard?

4   Write a heading 'The mysterious Spaniard'.
(a) Which of these words describe him?

> blind   deaf   dumb   dangerous
> kind   long-haired   Red Joe   rich

Copy the ones you choose. There are four.

(b) Now write three or four sentences about the mysterious Spaniard. The words you have copied will help you.

Chapter 21

Let's talk

Find the true sentence. Why is it true? Why are the other sentences not true?

(a) Red Joe and his companion found some treasure in the house.

(b) Red Joe and his companion were going to bury the money in the house.

(c) Red Joe and his companion left the treasure in the house.

Let's write

1   Write these sentences in the order in which they happened.

- Red Joe was worried when he found the boys' spades.
- They found a box full of gold coins.
- Red Joe and his companion took the treasure when they left the house.
- They lifted up a heavy stone and began digging a hole.
- He hurt his leg when a stair broke under him.
- Red Joe and his companion woke up.
- They wanted to bury it somewhere.

2   Copy this sentence and put in the apostrophes. (Hint:
     You should put in *three* apostrophes.)

     "Murrels men used to come here," Red Joes companion
     said. "Its theirs."

     Now look back to page 61 to check your work.

3   How did Red Joe know that somebody else had been in the
     house recently? Write the answer in your own words.

4   Tom and Huck were very frightened when Red Joe decided
     to go upstairs. Copy the sentences from page 62 that show
     you how frightened they were. You should copy *four*
     sentences only.

Chapter 22

Let's talk

Find the true sentence. Why is it true? Why are the other
sentences not true?
(a) Number Two was a room at Fred Miller's place.
(b) Tom unlocked the back door of Number Two.
(c) Tom wouldn't mind going back to Red Joe's room while he
     is there.

Let's write

1   Copy and complete these sentences with information from

the chapter.
  (a) For the last _____ years a young _____ had
       been staying in Room Number _____ at _____
       Inn.
  (b) Red _____ was staying in Room Number _____
       at _____ place.
  (c) _____ trod on Red Joe's _____ when he went
       into the room.

2   Copy each question with the correct answer from the box.

  (a) Where was the back door of Number Two?
  (b) What did Tom have in his pockets?
  (c) Where did Tom and Huck escape to?

> An old barn.
> In a side street.
> Old keys.

3   What was Huck's plan for getting the treasure from Red
    Joe? Write two or three sentences in your own words.

4   Look at the picture on page 65 and think about these
    questions.

    Who is the man on the floor? Why is he there? What has
    he got in his hand? What is Tom doing? Why was he
    frightened?

    Write a heading 'Tom's escape' and underneath write three
    or four sentences about what happened.

Chapter 23

Let's talk

Find the true sentence. Why is it true? Why are the other sentences not true?

(a) Huck called for Tom every night.
(b) Becky's mother told her to stay at Widow Douglas's.
(c) The children enjoyed the picnic.

Let's write

1 Choose the correct word from the brackets to complete each sentence. Copy the whole sentence.
   (a) Then Becky Thatcher came back (at, from, on) her holiday in the city.
   (b) Tom knew he (must, ought, should) to go back home that night.
   (c) Tom (decided, told, wanted) not to go home that night.

2 Copy and finish these sentences.
   (a) _____ because he was waiting for Huck to call him.
   (b) They did not go far into the cave because _____ .
   (c) Tom wanted to stay at Widow Douglas's because _____ .

3   Which of these can you find in the picture on page 67?

> cave   glass   jacket   jug
>
> plate   stool   treasure   teapot

Write down the ones you have found. There are four.

4   Copy and complete these questions by adding the correct question word.

(a) _____ was Huck going to call Tom? By making a "me-ow" sound.

(b) _____ did Mrs. Thatcher want Becky to stay with Susan Harper? So that she wouldn't be so tired.

(c) _____ did the children light their way in the cave? With candles.

Chapter 24

Let's talk

Find the true sentence. Why is it true? Why are the other sentences not true?

(a) Tom was in his hiding-place when the two men passed by.

(b) Red Joe was planning to harm Widow Douglas.

(c) Mr. Jones and his sons wouldn't help Huck.

Let's write

1 Match the beginnings of these sentences with the correct endings.

(a) Huck followed the men by himself   towards Widow Douglas's house.

(b) The men stopped   because there was no time to tell Tom.

(c) Red Joe had been sent to prison   outside Widow Douglas's house.

(d) The two men stood outside Widow Douglas's house   by Widow Douglas's husband.

(e) Mr. Jones and his sons ran   waiting for the lights to go out.

2 Here is the answer to a question:

Because he was quite near the men.

The question begins 'Why . . .?'. Now write the question and then copy the answer underneath.

3 Copy this paragraph and fill each space correctly with a word from the story.

After he had overheard what Red Joe was saying, Huck ran to Mr. _____ for help. He knocked at the _____ . Mr. _____ spoke to him from the _____ window and then came _____ with his two strong _____ .

They went to _____ _____ 's house. Huck heard a _____ , then he _____ away as fast as he could.

4   On page 69, Red Joe said:

"She'll look very pretty when I've finished with her."

He meant:

(a) "I am going to help her put on some make-up."
(b) "She will not look pretty after this."
(c) She will look very pretty when I stop seeing her."

Copy the one you choose.

Chapter 25

Let's talk

Find the true sentence. Why is it true? Why are the other sentences not true?

(a) Mr. Jones and his sons found the criminals in the woods.
(b) Huck told Mr. Jones that Red Joe was the Spaniard.
(c) Mr. Jones told Widow Douglas that Huck had saved her life.

Let's write

1   Copy each question with the correct answer from the box.

(a) What was the Spaniard like?

(b) What was the Spaniard's real name?
(c) What was the stranger like?

     Red Joe.

     He was tall and thin and he wore old clothes.

     He had long white hair and he was dumb.

2   Copy these words and underline the spelling mistake.

    breakfast   crinimals   excitement   promised

    Can you write the correct spelling too?

3   Mr. Jones and his sons were very surprised when they heard what Huck said about Red Joe. How did they show they were surprised? Copy the sentence that tells you on page 72.

4   Copy and finish these sentences.

    (a) Huck couldn't eat anything at breakfast because _____ _____ .

    (b) _____ when he saw a man carrying a heavy box.

    (c) Widow Douglas wanted to know what _____ .

Chapter 26

Let's talk

Find the true sentence. Why is it true? Why are the other sentences not true?

(a) Tom went to church on Sunday morning.
(b) Aunt Polly went to look for Tom in the cave.
(c) The men searched for the children for three days and three nights.

Let's write

1   Copy and finish these sentences with names from the chapter.

   (a) Everybody thought that _____ and _____ had lost their way in the cave.

   (b) _____ 's father, _____ _____ , led the men who were searching for the children.

   (c) _____ stayed at Mr. _____ 's house when he was ill and _____ _____ looked after him.

2   Copy this paragraph and fill each space correctly with a word from the box.

   Aunt Polly and Mrs. Thatcher were very worried _____ Tom and Becky had not come home after the picnic. The other children did not know _____ had happened to them. Everybody said the children were lost in the cave,

_____ the men began to look for them. The search went on for three days _____ the men found only the names "Tom" and "Becky" written on a rock. People thought _____ the children were dead.

| because | but | so | that | what |

3   Copy and complete these sentences with information from the chapter.

When Mrs. Thatcher felt ill:

   i) her face _____
   ii) _____ tremble
   iii) she _____

4   Think about the story, then copy this list and underline the odd one out.

books   candles   food   rope

Why is it the odd one out?

Chapter 27

Let's talk

Find the true sentence. Why is it true? Why are the other

sentences not true?

(a) Becky wasn't afraid of the dark.
(b) Becky stayed awake all the time.
(c) Red Joe was in the cave too.

Let's write

1 Write these sentences in the order in which they happened.

- They heard shouting.
- Tom and Becky decided to explore the cave.
- Tom saw Red Joe.
- They were frightened by bats.
- Tom tried to find the way out, using a piece of string as a guide.
- They finished their cake and the last candle went out.
- They lost their way.

2 Copy and complete these questions with a question word or question words.

(a) _____ was Becky's candle put out? By a bat flying at it.
(b) _____ cake did Tom give to Becky? Half.
(c) _____ couldn't they shout loudly? Because they were too weak.

3 Skim through the chapter to find words that mean nearly the same as:

(a) go and find out what is there

(b) out of breath
(c) went on

Write the words and phrases in order, to match (a), (b) and
(c) above.

4   Write a heading 'The piece of string' and think about these
     questions.

     Where did Tom keep the string? What did he do with it?
     Why was this a sensible idea? Did he find a way out of the
     cave? Did he give up?

     Now write three or four sentences about what happened.

Chapter 28

Let's talk

Find the true sentence. Why is it true? Why are the other
sentences not true?

(a) Tom and Becky were brought back to the village in the
     middle of the night.
(b) The men who had been searching for Tom and Becky
     found them in the cave.
(c) Red Joe stabbed himself.

Let's write

1   Match the beginnings of these sentences with the correct

endings.

   (a) Tom and Becky came back   with an iron door.
       to the village

   (b) Tom explained   when Tom went to see
                                         him.

   (c) Two men in a boat brought   in the cave.
       Tom and Becky

   (d) Huck was still sick in bed   in an open carriage.

   (e) Judge Thatcher closed the   back to the village.
       cave

   (f) Red Joe died   how they got out of the
                                         cave.

2   Copy these sentences and fill each space with the correct word from the box.

   (a) There was Aunt Polly, _____ face was shining like the sun.

   (b) Tom went to see Huck, _____ was still sick in bed.

   (c) 'Red Joe' was the name _____ made the boys tremble.

> that   who   whose

3   Choose the correct word from the brackets to complete each sentence. Copy the whole sentence.

   (a) The men had (been, looked, searched) the cave in vain.

(b) All the village (gathered, reached, went) at Judge Thatcher's house.

(c) Widow Douglas was still (caring, looking, taking) after Huck.

4 Write a heading 'Red Joe' and think about these questions.

Where was the iron door put? Why was this bad for Red Joe? How did he die? Why? Where was his body found?

Now write three or four sentences about what happened.

Chapter 29

Let's talk

Find the true sentence. Why is it true? Why are the other sentences not true?

(a) Tom and Huck found Red Joe's treasure in the cave.

(b) The treasure was hidden in a big bag.

(c) Mr. Jones went to the cave to meet the two boys.

Let's write

1 Copy this paragraph and fill each space correctly with a word from the box.

Tom and Huck wanted to find Red Joe's _____ . They thought it was in the _____ . When they got into the cave, they found the _____ that marked

where the treasure was. They started digging and soon
struck something hard. It was a _____ full of gold
_____ . Because it was so heavy, the _____ filled
their _____ with the coins. Then they rowed back to
the _____ and borrowed a _____ from Mr. Jones.

| bags | box | boys | cart | cave | coins |
| cross | treasure | village | | | |

2   Copy and finish these sentences.

(a) Tom and Huck stopped being afraid of Red Joe after

_____ .

(b) Tom held up his candle so that _____ .

(c) The two boys began to laugh and sing and dance when

_____ .

3   Write these words in alphabetical order.

spades   string   bags   matches   candles

4   Choose the best title for the paragraph beginning 'The two
boys started digging . . .' on page 82.

(a) Looking for treasure
(b) Digging for treasure
(c) Finding treasure

Copy the one you choose.

Chapter 30

Let's talk

Find the true sentence. Why is it true? Why are the other sentences not true?

(a) Widow Douglas gave Tom and Huck a good wash.
(b) Tom and Huck did not like Sid.
(c) Tom was going to keep all the treasure for himself.

Let's write

1 Copy these sentences and fill each space with a word from the box.

   (a) Widow Douglas kissed the boys _____ they came in.
   (b) "We won't begin _____ you're ready."
   (c) Everyone looked _____ they could hardly believe what they saw.

but	till	when

2 Copy these sentences and put in the three apostrophes that have been left out. (Don't look back at the chapter yet!)

   (a) Sid looked at the boys dirty clothes.
   (b) "Half of it is Hucks and half of it is mine," Tom explained.

(c) Tom told the story of Red Joes treasure.

3   Widow Douglas was going to help Huck. Copy the things
     she offered to do.

   ● Give him a bath.
   ● Give him a home.
   ● Look after him like a mother.
   ● Send him to school.
   ● Send him to college.
   ● Find some work for him.

4   Look at the picture on page 85 and think about these
     questions.

     Where are all the people? Why are they surprised? What
     has Tom emptied on to the table? Who did it belong to?
     Who does it belong to now? Will it change their lives.?

     Now write a heading 'The treasure' and underneath write
     three or four sentences about what happened.

Chapter 31

Let's talk

Find the true sentence. Why is it true? Why are the other sentences not true?

(a) More treasure was found in the village.
(b) Tom found Huck beside the river.
(c) Tom persuaded Huck to go back to Widow Douglas.

Let's write

1   Huck was not happy a Widow Douglas's. Copy and complete this list of reasons why he was unhappy there.

    i)He had _____ early.
   ii)_____ with a knife and fork.
  iii)_____ people.
  iv)_____ school.
   v)_____ clothes.
  vi_____ wash _____ .
 vii)_____ comb _____ .
viii)He was not allowed to _____ .
  ix) _____ go out at night.

2   Copy these sentences and fill each space with 'who' or 'where'.

    (a) Judge Thatcher put their money in a bank _____ it would be safe.

    (b) It was Tom _____ found him at last.

    (c) After three weeks, Huck ran away _____ nobody could find him.

3   Here is the answer to a question:

       Because it would be safe there.

The question begins 'Why . . .?'. Now write the question and then copy the answer underneath.

4   Write a heading 'Tom's band' and think about these questions.

What was the band going to do? What sort of boys could join the band? Was Tom going to let Huck join the band?

Now write three sentences about the band.